KINK CAMP

HUNTED

A. ANDERS

Copyright © 2022 by Adriana Anders

All rights reserved.

Cover image used under license from Canva.com

No part of this book may be reproduced in any form or by any electronic or mechanical means, including information storage and retrieval systems without written permission from the author, except for the use of brief quotations in a book review.

This is a work of fiction. Names, characters, businesses, places, events, locales, and incidents are either the products of the author's imagination or used in a fictitious manner. Any resemblance to actual persons, living or dead, or actual events is purely coincidental.

All brand names and product names in this book are trademarks, registered trademarks, or trade names of their respective holders. The author is not associated with any product or vendor in this book.

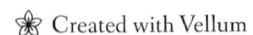

❦ Created with Vellum

ALSO BY ADRIANA ANDERS

Camp Haven/Kink Camp Series
Possession

Paris Je t'Aime Series
We'll Never Have Paris

The French Kiss-Off (coming soon)

The Survival Instincts Series
Deep Blue

Whiteout

Uncharted

Love at Last Series
Loving the Secret Billionaire

Loving the Wounded Warrior

Loving the Mountain Man

The Blank Canvas Series
Under Her Skin

By Her Touch

In His Hands

Standalone

Daddy Crush

ABOUT KINK CAMP

My desires…

I'm afraid. I want things – to escape, to run, to be caught, held down and…

I've come here to find the thing to quench my most sensual fantasies.

When I see him - I know. He's brutal and made of stone. An artist with his hands who keeps everyone at arm's length. He's the one I want – I need.

May be my downfall.

I'm not a man you play with. I gave up on finding a partner years ago.

But now I see her. Innocent. Beautiful. Temptation. I want to possess her as much as I want to protect her from myself.

I am the king here, but once she's gone? I'll be a man alone once again.

Now that I have her. I have to find a way to keep her – forever.

Camp Haven is a world apart, a place where pain is pleasure, hate can be love, and we are all our own true selves. Every act is consensual, every person respected —unless that's not what they want. This book plunges you into the deep end with, forced fantasy and primal play. Tread carefully.

To Lou.
I couldn't have asked for a better guide.

CONTENT WARNING AND AUTHOR'S NOTE

Content Warning: Camp Haven is a world apart, a place where pain is pleasure, hate can be love, and we are all our own true selves. Every act is consensual, every person respected—unless that's not what they want. This book plunges you into the deep end, with consensual non-consent, forced fantasy, and primal play. Tread carefully. Please note that there are mentions of cancer and other illness, along with trauma relating to the loss of a spouse.

Dear Reader,

Several years ago, I was lucky enough to go to a camp like the one I describe in this book. I've fictionalized that here, adding things and changing others for the sake of the story, though I've done my best to bring the heart of the experience to the page.

What I found most remarkable about the camp I attended was how absolutely happy people were to be there. There was none of the awkwardness I'd assumed I might find at a camp centered around BDSM and sex. In fact, if I had to compare the overall ambiance to anything, it would be to a joyous picnic—outdoors, free, open, consensual, non-judgmental. I wish the world were more like that camp. I wish I could go back there every summer, not for the sexy times, but for the overall delight of seeing people so in their elements—so happy, free, real.

My hope is that I've brought that to the page in this book. I want to give readers a taste of a world in which the only shame is the kind the characters ask for. My ultimate goal with the Camp Haven series is to give my readers an escape that's safe, sane, consensual, and one hell of a good time.

Happy reading!

Adriana

1

Grace

***Male Primal Hunter** seeks Female Prey for a one-time, anonymous hunt.*
No faces. No names. No repeats.

I GO STILL the moment I see the ad.

Around me, people chat and laugh. Someone whooshes by in full on bondage gear, a throuple moans in the corner, a seven foot woman in a gold wrestling singlet steams milk behind the counter, and I barely notice any of it.

It's just a piece of paper, fluttering on the

message board in the camp coffee shop. One kinky request amongst dozens. But in my mind, it's a beacon, so clearly meant for me that it might as well spell out my name in bright, flashing neon.

I read it again, focusing on each word. Primal. That one alone sends excitement shimmering through me. And Prey. I swallow hard at that, feel it in my bones.

"So what do you think, Gracie? Should we do the workshop on sounding or the one on sex without orgasm?" My best friend Max asks, sounding a million miles away. "I hear Mistress Quest is amazing, so I'm leaning towards sounding, but it might be a bit much for you on your first—" Apparently noticing that I'm no longer by her side, she stops and turns. "Uh, Grace?"

I'd answer, but I'm stuck in front of this ad, a thousand familiar fantasies running through my brain. In them, I'm sprinting, breathing hard, scared, but not terrified. Not really. I mean, there's a little fear underneath it all, but that's just part of the thrill. I hide, turn to look back, see nothing. But he's there. He's always there. And, in my dreams, he catches me. He takes what he—

"Grace! What are you..." Max follows the direction of my gaze. "Oh." Her eyes widen as they slide to me, then back to the ad. "Oooooooh."

Because she's Max and she's fearless and never hesitates, she reaches out and tears the thing down.

"I don't think you're supposed to do that," I tell her, rule follower that I am.

With one of those scrunched up expressions that says, *Whatever, Gracie*, she slides her arm through mine and drags me along. "So," she says as we join the coffee line. "You gonna do it?"

"I don't know." I'm buzzing inside, every part of me worked up, screaming *Yes, yes, do it!* "Maybe?" I can't stop staring at the ad. We should put it back so he doesn't get mad. Then again, what's he gonna do? Punish me? The idea shimmers through me, half dread, half excitement.

"You totally should."

The person in front of us grabs their coffee and throws us a smile as they head over to the cream and sugar station. They're wearing nothing but full body sparkle paint and knee-high combat boots. Not a stitch of actual clothing. Max gives them an easy wave, but I can't quite meet their eye. After spending a week at Camp Haven every summer for the last five years, she's an old hand at this. I, however, still don't know where to look.

"Mad Max!" The towering amazon behind the counter squeals.

"Lamé! You look amazing!" Max and the barista exchange a long, tight hug over the counter. When they're done, Max wraps an arm around me. "This is Grace. My best friend in the entire world. I finally convinced her to come to camp."

"You a hugger?" At my quiet *Sure*, Lamé leans over and engulfs me in her jasmine-infused embrace before letting me go. "Welcome to Camp Haven, honey! How do you like it so far?"

"It's…" I can't find a word to describe how absolutely different this place is from anything I've experienced. Everyone here is unique, so unabashedly themselves that as just myself, I feel almost like a fraud. Lamé, for example, is rocking the wrestling singlet, which outlines perky nipples and shows off a dusting of scarlet curls at the neckline. Her coppery skin and perfectly straight black hair remind me of Morticia Adams, an impression that's only reinforced by the wicked gleam in her eyes. The bracelets on her arm tell me her pronouns (she/her/they/them), that she's a Dominant, into power exchange, and in a relationship, but open to other partners. "Amazing," I finish with an admiring smile.

Lamé looks around at the coffee shop's occupants. "Isn't it?" With a sigh, she turns back to us. "What can I get you two?"

We order and I zone out while Lamé works the big espresso machine like a maestro, her long, sparkly nails tapping out a mesmerizing rhythm.

Really, though, I'm thinking about that piece of paper in Max's hand.

"Hey, Lamé, what do you know about this?" Max reads my mind. "Think it's legit?" She flattens the ad out on the counter.

Lamé turns, mid-steam, catches sight of the ad and crinkles her face at Max. "I didn't know you were a Primal."

"Not for me."

Lamé's eyes move to me and narrow, one bright red eyebrow lifting. "Oh, yeah?" She drops what she's doing and slides back over to the bar, squinting at me so hard I begin to squirm. "You gonna respond?"

I start to shrug and then stop myself. I didn't come here to watch from the sidelines. I came here to let myself live, to find myself. To be myself.

To stop hiding.

"I'm thinking about it," I say, unable to keep my chin from rising.

"You know him? The Primal?" Max asks.

"I might." Glossy lips pursed, Lamé tilts her head, never looking away from me.

"Is it safe?" Max prods, ever the protector. And even if I'm way too old for this level of shielding, I love her for it. I'll *always* love her for how much she cares about me. "I mean, is he trustworthy?"

"He's the best man I know. Nobody safer." Lamé finally breaks eye contact to glance at Max, before coming back to me. "And nobody more dangerous." She's deadly serious.

The shiver that rolls through me is big and delicious, inviting goosebumps and stiff nipples and a sigh I barely manage to cover up with a cough.

Lamé, I can tell, sees right through it. She knows

I'm turned on by the idea of a stranger in the woods, the danger, the anonymity. The loss of power. "Wow," is all I manage to say, but I guess it's enough for her.

She smirks and leans forward to whisper above the music, "He's so hot, honey. If I was into getting hunted down and fucked in the woods, this is the man I'd want to do it." She shakes herself with a shimmy that sends her earrings rattling like wind chimes, and turns with a flourish to finish making our drinks.

I suck in a breath, look down at the ad again, and reread every single word, slowly. Carefully. Max is probably watching me, but I need a second to regroup.

This ad is so up my alley, it's as if the man who wrote it pulled it straight from my brain. It's absolutely, one hundred percent my fantasy and it has been for as long as I can remember, though I've never followed through on it before.

Well, maybe a little bit, when I was a kid. Like the time I begged Tommy Moore to tackle me in a game of tag during fourth grade recess and he did and then I thought my heart would explode from how his weight felt on me. Or the thing where Caroline from next door would come over and we'd play a version of hide-and-seek that culminated in torture sessions in my closet and somehow I was always the victim and she the eternal tormentor and I could never, ever get enough of that moment when she wrapped her hand around my arm and told me to lie down. Even now, the memory has me squeezing my thighs together, although it's not so much the memory as the rough, slightly wrinkled feel of this paper between my fingers and the knowledge that the real thing's right here, within reach.

My vision's a little hazy when I turn to Max and say, "Okay," in a voice that's rough and out of breath. "I want to do it."

"Yeah?" Max watches me so closely I have to wrap my arms around myself to keep her from seeing the effects this talk's had on my body. "You sure?"

I nod just as Lamé sets our cups in front of us, the steam adding to the haze in my head.

"I've never had an orgasm." For some reason, the words are out before I can catch them. At the look of complete shock on Lamé's face, I go on. "With a partner, I mean. With a guy. A man. Anyone."

Lamé exchanges a look with Max. "You've come to the right place." She claps her hands, then spins and glides down to grab something at the other end of the counter. Only now do I realize she's wearing roller skates. "Okay." She slaps a couple forms down on the bar. "I need you to fill in this release, along with the other paper. This just gives you a chance to give us your hard and soft limits, and other things. Camp staff will set things up. It's all very confidential. Especially given wh—" She shuts her mouth hard and covers up whatever she'd been about to let slip with a grin. "Here's a pen, honey."

We move to a table and I fill in the form as best I can, with answers like Yes for Oral and, after some hesitation, No for Anal, although it's something I'd consider in the future. I jot down the camp's safe words and end with a short paragraph describing my fantasy as completely as I can. It's the first time I've written any of it down, which feels both wrong, after keeping it locked up for so long, and absolutely freeing.

The release form confirms that the camp staff is aware of the session and either person can tap out at any time. The play area will be safe and secure. Only the appropriate people will be allowed within the cordoned off zone, and security will remain near the scene, but out of the way. Under emergency number, I put Max, obviously, not my mom. The form's reassuring and scary and it normalizes the whole thing in a way that brings me close to tears, after so many years of repression and shame at what my mind and body seem to want. By the time I'm done, I'm as drained as the cup of coffee beside me.

Finally, Max, who's chatted with other people to give me privacy, walks me back up to the counter. Good thing, because Lamé's next words almost knock my legs out from under me.

"You free tonight?"

Oh my God. This is happening.

I swallow and glance at Max. She nods.

"Yes. Yeah. I'm free tonight."

"Good, honey." Lamé hands me a handwritten

note card, showing a time and place, along with a set of basic rules underscoring the other person's desire for anonymity. I shove it in my pocket so the others can't see how hard my hand's shaking. "Better get ready," she says with a grin and a wink and a little wave goodbye. "Cause it's game on."

2

Grace

You know those montages in movies, where people laughingly get a makeover or go on a picnic or fall in love in the space of one song? The day doesn't go by like that—at all. In fact, my day's probably the polar opposite of that. It's endless and surreal, filled with jittery images of strangers doing strange things to each other. That's just kink camp, I guess, but while it fascinated me when I arrived yesterday, right now, it's just too much. Too much screaming and pain and pleasure. Too many easy smiles and naked bodies, too many sounds and sights and smells that remind me of what I've agreed to do tonight. I can barely eat at lunch or dinner, which means Max pushes food at me every time I head back to our fancy glamp site—otherwise known as the Thunderdome. She won't let me drink, though.

"Camp Rules," she says, plugging in the twinkle lights that make this spot the homiest.

The sun's almost down and my nerves are so lit up I could scream. "I read the rules, Max. I'm allowed two drinks before a scene." Ignoring her, I pull a hard cider from the cooler, take a couple long swallows and set it down. Yeah. That's not the greatest idea. All it's doing is making my belly feel wrong.

I should listen to Max. She's the expert here. I'm just the childhood bestie she's dragged to camp, after years of trying to get me to come with. See, Max is unabashedly kinky. She's open and without shame or complex. I've always loved that about her. I, on the other hand, stuffed my fantasies so deep inside for so long that my libido's been...I won't say dormant. I have sex, I mean. I have relationships. And they're... fine. But life's been hard. My dreams have sort of dissipated. Pleasure doesn't seem all that important when the day-to-day is such a struggle.

I like sex. I do. I've just never felt overcome by it. I want to feel that.

Ever since I admitted to Max this fantasy that I have—what, maybe four years ago?—she's been begging me to get involved in this community and, above all, to come to camp.

I tried to tell my ex about my fantasy a couple

months ago, which led him to break up with me. It knocked me flat on my ass. Then Mom's doc had the audacity to agree with Mom when she mentioned that I looked tired and stressed and needed a vacation.

So, here I am. Ready to give it a try. It's probably not exactly what Mom—or the nosy doctor—meant by *vacation*, but hey. I'm here, right?

"You know what?" I tell Max. "I'm just gonna go."

"I'll walk you."

"No." I lift a hand, giving her a smile to soften the refusal. "I need to do this on my own. Like, you know, to get into it, I guess."

"Oh, right. I can see that. Like, walk alone and get all…"

What's she gonna say? Creeped out? Scared? Horny? I don't think any of those are right, but I do know I need a transition of some sort between this real life I've always lived and the fantasy I'm finally diving into. "Acclimated," I finally tell her. From her knowing smile, I can tell the therapist in her loves that. "Later, gator."

"Whatever, crocodile."

I wave and smile and start down the path that leads into the quickly darkening woods and the designated spot. It's my second time heading over there today. The first gave me a chance to check out the scene, sort of envision it, and also make sure I could run around without, you know, tripping on branches, or falling into a pile of poison ivy. What I noticed was, though the spot he's selected is wooded, it's been entirely cleared of underbrush. There's not a single poison ivy leaf, much less a stone to trip on or a low-hanging branch to run into. Whoever's in charge here really knows what they're doing.

That attention to detail, probably more than anything else, calms me as I walk past a group of people singing show tunes around a campfire that provides my last glimmer of artificial light.

There's no moon tonight to light my way through the trees. When the sun sets entirely, it'll be pitch black.

That's what he wants.

I force myself to take deep, measured breaths and slow my pace. It smells like campfires out here. Like safety.

Turning around, I remind myself, is still an option. It's always an option.

Still, I go forward, placing one foot, then the other. Marching towards this fate I've chosen.

The sound of spanking and laughter and singing fades into the background, replaced by the chirping of insects and the crunch of my feet on leaves. It smells different here. Like pine needles and rot. I pass a person wearing an orange arm band, who nods and then ignores me. Security.

This is it.

I get the wildest urge to call out, like the first one to die in a horror movie, and then, because this is it—

this is *my* fantasy, dammit—I open my mouth and do it. "Hello?" My voice is lost to the night sky, soaked up by rough bark and damp ground and the calls of a million little creatures. I don't know why, but suddenly, I need to be heard, by *him*. "Anybody here?" I make the shaky words carry this time and, God, it's weird, but I think he hears me. I think he likes it.

A stick breaks to my right and I jump, not quite holding in a squeak.

He's heard me.

Oh, shit. I can't breathe. I'm going to hyperventilate. My belly's a mess of right and wrong and what the fuck am I doing? Forcing myself to stop, I shut my eyes and slow it all down—the fear and excitement blasting through my veins, the chaotic mess in my mind.

Another footfall, closer this time. The sound so definite, so clear that it centers me.

I have one job here. One. It's to run. Run and get caught and—

No, just run. He'll do the rest.

Ready...Set...

I take off like my life depends on it, like there's nothing but the rhythm of thrumming blood in my veins, the slap of my feet to the uneven ground, the harsh scrub of air over my dry, tight throat.

The dark's closing in. Branches come out of nowhere, roots trip me up. My lungs burn way too fast.

He's back there, his footfalls loud and careless. This monster's not sneaking around, trying to be quiet. He thrashes and pounds, breaks through whatever's in his way.

Holy shit, maybe I don't want to do this. Do I want this? Is it a mistake? It's a mistake.

Red! It flashes through my mind. A stoplight, not the word. I should say it. I could. Red Red Red.

No. No, I *want* to do this. I'm doing this.

The knowledge lands hard between my legs and in my stomach. I feel sick and horny and lost out here in the woods.

I throw my hand out, smack a tree, go right, almost run into another tree, and slow down, hands out wide now. Another tree. Where is he? Where is he?

I change directions and move on. My wild inner animal pushes me deeper and deeper into the living, breathing, damp moss chaos of the woods. Insects hit my face, a vine grabs my foot and sends me flailing to the ground. I'm up fast, barely cringing at the way my shoulder aches. He's close now. So close I want to look back.

My outstretched palm scrapes rough bark—a wide tree. I stop. Cling to it, like a lifeline. Will he see me back here? How small can I make myself? Pulling my limbs in tight, I shut my eyes, quiet my breath and listen.

Should I look? I need to look, the way I do in the fantasy, when I rub my clit and let my inner self fly.

Hardly moving at all, I peek out, just the barest bit.

Oh, shit. Shit, shit, shit.

He's right there.

I push forward again. Arms wrapped around my head for protection. I put on speed, thighs aching. My foot bumps something and I lurch, right myself, keep going. Oh, fuck, my toe. I shut out the pain.

I think about his silhouette. It was huge. Big enough to blot out more than his share of the night sky. I'm not small, but I am nothing compared to that mass.

There's no stopping the whimpering coming from me. It's the animal.

I'm prey. Just prey.

My leg knocks into something hard. I trip, sailing forward, hands braced to take the brunt of it. *I told you so.* Quick as lightning, I see the ER visit, a cast, no work, explanations. Pain, pain, pain. One hand hits the ground.

And then I just...stop.

3

Grace

All the air gets knocked out of me. Not from the fall. There's an arm around my waist.

I grunt, hover above the ground for a millisecond, like someone out of *The Matrix*, and rise up, stunned when my back smacks into a wide, hard surface.

It's his chest. His other arm wraps around me. Thick, warm muscles. Skin hot against mine.

He walks us forward a few steps, my feet dangling above the forest floor. We stop. He shoves me toward a tree, brusque, violent, but painless.

The arms let go and his whole big body moves in, traps me against deeply rutted bark.

I struggle. Wild, frantic, lost. All I can do is shake

myself like a dog, limbs scrabbling, pushing back and back, then to the side. I need out. I need out. Anything. Anything to get away and—

One callused hand collars my throat. The other tightens in my hair. The threat's so much more than I'd ever pictured from my safe, soft bed.

"Please don't do this."

A few silent seconds pass and awareness slips in. I don't remember wrapping my hand against his wrist, but I'm holding him tightly. We're pressed together, like we know each other. His palm cups my neck. My pulse races light and high and he must feel it. Can he?

Can he tell that I still want this?

My chest moves, expanding to press my breasts to the tree, then contracting. He must feel that. My back's tight to his front and he's hot. My God, his chest is pouring out heat like an oven. It should be uncomfortable in this hot summer night, but I like it. It feels...

Fuck, is it weird to say safe?

That's exactly it, though. I've been taken down, trapped, held. I sink into this loss of control.

My mouth works at the sudden idea that I could use the safe word again. Would he stop if I did?

Yes. I'm sure of it. This man, who's holding me prisoner without inflicting an ounce of pain, would stop. It's the last thing I want.

"Quit fighting," he grates out, his voice no more than a whisper.

I kick out. I can't help it. I'm stubborn like that.

He tightens his hold. I'm ensnared, my head dragged back against his neck.

Oh, oh God, I smell him here. Musk. Sweat. I suck in a desperate breath. He's basic, mineral, earthy. The smell of him punches me low in the belly, mixing fear and guilt and lust into a cocktail I could drown in.

I want to drown.

His smell's good. It feels right, unlike my ex Dean and my boyfriend before him. Every gasp is full of him and me and the raw earth smell.

A hot tear slides down my face.

My nipples are hard, my breasts aching. "Let me go," I force out, as close to a whisper as I can manage.

"Shhhhh." He leans into me and, sweet Jesus, his cock's a hard, huge brand against my back. He's rough and he's mean and he's going to fuck me and then walk away. That's *exactly* what I want. "Stay very still and it won't hurt."

The desire's so strong that it does hurt. My body's too swollen, too aching, too tense.

He's already let go of my hair to work at the front of my jeans, using his weight to pin me to the tree. I don't even feel the desire to move, but more than that, I want him to pin me in place.

And then I buck, because I can. I shriek at the feel of his other hand at my neckline. He fists the fabric, stretches it down over my breast, dragging the top of my bra cup with it. Shock tingles in my fingers, my toes, the painful point of my nipple. Those rough fingers pinch me there, sending sparks to every cell in my body.

I'm so wet I want to sob. Aching and empty and squirming with want that only gets worse when his fingers wind through my pubic hair and give my curls a good, hard tug.

"Oh, fuck." I don't even try to whisper. Disguising my voice worked when I had brain cells. That's a thing of the past.

He shushes me, ramping up my humiliation, and tugs my jeans over my hips.

This is actually happening. I mean, it's obvious. I know. The penetration, though.

The orgasm.

Moaning, I push back, my ass wriggling in invitation.

This guy's an asshole, though, whoever he is. He knows that I want it. That I'm close to begging for that big cock I felt against my back.

It only slows him down, makes him draw things out. He's a tiger toying with me when he pulls my other cup down and slaps my bare breast.

And I'm cornered, just like I wanted. No agency. No choice but to take it.

I lean my forehead on the trunk and try to see something. His hands, if not his face. "Please." I don't know why I say it. "Please."

All I can make out are dim shapes: my breasts, hanging crudely down, his hand switching painfully from one to the other, forcing ugly, soul-deep grunts into the air.

He shifts back, grabs both nipples and twists. I swear I go feral, howling or baying or, hell, I don't know, communing with the moon.

Something changes. I whimper, try to turn. He holds me down with a hand to the back of my head. "Don't move."

I *can't* move like this. "Please." Pleasure zaps from my core to my limbs. God, please.

He does something behind me. The condom. I hear the rip and rustle, the smooth hum of a zipper, the plastic snap of the thing going on.

It's all happening slowly, and fast. Too quickly for me to latch onto details. I want them, though. I want to bottle it all up for later.

He's efficient in the dark. Not his first rodeo. The most absurd spike of jealousy pierces my skin like a splinter.

Before I can unpack that, he's got my hip in his grip, he runs that hand down my front and finally— God, finally—he gets to my sopping wet core.

A growl rumbles out into the night, low and deep, so quiet it's almost a purring in his chest.

My pussy clenches, my whole body tense with expectation. I think he likes how tense I've gotten. His fingers sweep down, slow and easy, splaying my lips before glancing my clit. His gentle slap forces a gasp from my lungs.

Without warning, he bends at the knee, urges my

hips back, and slides his thick cock between my thighs. It's so sudden, my mind stutters.

He's thick. Fuck, thick and hot.

One long, slick glide forward, another back. The sound of his erection through all that wetness is obscene and embarrassing and I want to curl in on myself and hide.

He won't let me. Of course not.

Another easy glide of his cock between my legs, the threat of penetration, the promise of something else. I've never been so turned on in my life. Every move, sound, smell is right here.

His crown notches at my entrance.

I freeze.

We're just two animals, in the wild. One toying with the other, threatening, though only gently. I'm at his mercy, waiting.

Wanting. Aching with need.

Empty.

Is he teasing me? Has he changed his mind?

I reach for him then, which I guess is a mistake. The second my hand touches his erection, he goes absolutely wild.

And good lord I did not know what I was getting into.

4

G race

My body moves back, the change so abrupt, I see stars. I slam into him, the tree suddenly gone. I'm a helpless mess—legs caught in my jeans, breasts out, ass buck naked in the woods.

"Don't fucking touch me," he snarls, right into my ear. A split second later, I'm lowered face down to the ground, his body above, then on top of me and...

Oh fuck. He's on me, his cock and pubic hair grinding against my cunt. He's rasping out breaths that heat my neck, my ear, my shoulder.

It's terrifying and yet I speak this language. My body wants this.

I claw for something—his hair—and get a handful

of fabric. He grasps my hand and yanks it away with a harsh, "No."

It takes me a second to realize it's a ski mask. He's wearing a mask. Of course he is.

"Don't touch that."

"Sorry." I'm, breathless, eager. *Don't stop.*

My body wants more of this—the fight. Twisting, I work to get him off me. Something primitive's building inside me, scratching and scrabbling to get out. I can't grab his hair, but I can push him. I can twist hard and use my knees.

He grunts and reacts, bigger, more brutal.

This. This savage, bestial thing. This is what I want. What I need.

We scuffle in the dirt. My forearm blocks him, cuts him off at the throat. He grunts and gives me his weight. It's as much of a tool as his blunt hands.

Why am I fighting this? I honestly don't know. I don't know why it feels so right to shove an elbow in his side or twist hard in his grasp. I like it when he traps me, too. Hands on my wrists, legs pegging mine to the cool, mossy earth.

Oh, fuck, his erection's right there and I'm so turned on it hurts.

Everything hurts.

"Don't fucking move," he grunts.

I follow rules, I don't break them. Why don't I listen?

My inner animal's too fierce to go gentle into this

good night. With a snarl of my own, I twist, hard, truly trying to escape. He counters.

I crawl maybe two feet before he's over me, on me, constricting my world into heat and breath, beastly sounds and the damp smell of soil. He's too fast, too strong, too dominant.

I'm so wet, it's slicking down my thighs. I can smell it, mingled with the rich loam of dead leaves and new growth and... Oh, oh, oh my body's arching up to him, inviting him in while still trying to claw away. My ass is beckoning, my legs straining to open where he's kept me clamped together.

I crane my head—not to escape this time, but to turn and, hell, I don't know, kiss him, maybe? Bite him? I strain to see behind his mask, watch his body, take in the size of the monster who's overpowered me.

"Anything you want to say?" This, I know, is my last chance to give the safe word.

I shut my mouth, shake my head.

"Good." He nudges my ear with his nose and breathes in, though I wonder how much he can smell through that mask. "Good girl." Goosebumps race over my body, painful as the empty ache between my legs. I stretch myself out, an offering to the beast.

He responds with a firm press of his hips.

Slowly, almost lazily now, he pulls back enough to push the hot length of his erection between my thighs. Taking his time, he slides a hand under my abdomen and lifts me higher, angling me the way he likes.

I can't move. I don't want to. I'm staying right here. It feels elemental and dirty. And free.

Being ground into the mud, half-naked, alone with a stranger, I feel more right than I have in years.

He's making muted, gruff sounds, more barbarian than man. He thrusts against my folds, hitting my clit. I shudder. I think I groan. I don't know.

My body takes his movements, curves into them.

We've danced this way before. The thought comes and goes.

When he wedges the thick, blunt crown of his cock to my entrance this time, I whine with relief, fear, pure, pure want, real life so far from my mind I might as well not even have a name.

I couldn't give it right now if I tried.

One side of my face is flush to the ground, my ass in the air, my nipples skimming the earth's surface as he presses harder, deeper, his erection bigger than I'm used to, his body heftier, bossier, mean as all hell.

I'm pliable, but not weak. Even in this state I know he's fought for this. We both have. Fuck, it's so good.

The way he works himself into me, slowly, inexorably, I feel taken, one slow inch after another, full of him by the time he's in to the hilt. And then, when that's not enough, I buck back and, goddamn, he wraps me up in his solid frame, wedging me to him with his chin on my shoulder, his toes under mine.

I'm his. I'm so definitely, solidly his, that I sigh. I just sigh and press back in search of pleasure now, not distance. My body's giving and holding, going loose and tense and open to absolutely anything—anything—anything at all.

He hugs me tighter, pulls out and thrusts in again, hitting something high and bright inside me that scares me with its intensity. Another slick outward slide, another deep, heavy thrust. Another, another. I'm keening almost continuously, my hips working with his, my front grinding itself into the ground in search of friction. I've never felt so swollen and ripe, never imagined how pleasurable the rough scrub of grit could be. Against my cheek, my breasts.

As if he's in my brain, he plucks a nipple, hard. Everything inside me contracts. Pleasure's a spinning, strobing thrum, knotting up so tight it's all I can think of. A need so strong I'd do anything in the world to get there. I've never been this wound up with a partner, never felt this close to the edge.

He pumps inside, hitting that place again, and I don't care how any of this will feel tomorrow. Hell, I welcome the bruises, the scrapes, the cuts. I want to be this broken thing, rubbed raw.

His fingers slide between my legs, skate over my lips to my clit. It's absolutely electrified. It doesn't take much. A few flicks, a quick pinch, and I'm there—

No, not there—*here*. Everywhere.

Fuck, I'm exploding. He's pumping into me hard, close to the end for him, I think, and all I can do is fall into sensation the way you dive into water, head first.

Completely. Giving myself up to it. And that initial moment, like breaking below the surface, is utterly empty. No thought, no sensation beyond pure, endless bliss.

I feel nothing. It's wonderful.

Coming down is the hard part. I knew it would be, but I had no idea just how bad. It's like a drug, I imagine, although I've got nothing to compare it to.

I'm shaky, a little lost, and cold, despite his enveloping warmth. I shiver, which I don't imagine he'll notice, seeing as how he just orgasmed inside me. In the condom, I mean, but still. He surprises me by rubbing a hand up my arm to my shoulder, then back down again. Our palms meet, mine squeezes, he squeezes me back.

Okay then. That's it. I've done it. I mean... Jesus. This is it. What I wanted. All of it, from the set-up, to the chase, to my first-ever orgasm with a man was perfect. I want...

I shiver again, hating myself for wanting something, anything. And then, because I'm not allowed to need more than this—and not just based on his rules, but my own as well—I clear my throat, sniff, lift my head from the ground, and force out something approaching a laugh.

"I could use a drink."

His body shakes once, as if he's laughing too, though really, who can say? I mean, everything's been in my head, hasn't it? He's told me nothing.

And that's the way I want it. No complications, no strings. I came to camp for this very thing: to live out my fantasy. To have an orgasm with another person. Not once did I imagine I'd actually achieve any of it.

It's a toss up at this point as to whether I can walk, much less get up, but I've got to get out of here. I have to.

I lean back, showing him with my body that it's time to move and the guy, who can clearly take a hint, pulls out, leaving me achingly empty. He gets up. I have no idea if he offers me a hand. I use the tree, taking stock as I edge toward standing.

Oh, that's all gonna hurt tomorrow. Or tonight, actually. Good thing I don't sleep on my front. I brush dirt off my boobs, which feel as tender as these fresh emotions. I almost laugh at the idea of trying to explain cuts and bruises to the guys on the job site come Monday. *Nah, I'm good. Just busted my lip getting fucked by some rando in the woods. So, how's about them Cavs?*

Yeah, no. Much better keeping Randy and José in the dark about this week's activities. My colleagues are overprotective enough as it is. They'd lose it.

A little steadier, I pull the bra down, trying to ignore the sound his pants and zipper make. I don't even think he took his shirt off, so getting clothed again's easy for him. Him. The stranger. My stranger.

He hands me a sandal. I thank him. He doesn't reply.

Right. Anonymity. That was the big one for him. Makes me wonder who he is, of course. *Like, are you famous? Do you have a girlfriend?*

Dean—that asshole—broke up with me the day after I told him about the things that turn me on. *Too freaky*, he wrote in his break-up text. A *text!* We were talking about getting married, dammit. But sex with him wasn't anywhere close to this. It was mechanical. Almost a duty. All I feel about the break-up now is relief.

Crap, what am I doing even thinking about this? It's time to get out of here, leave this whole thing behind, get back to the campsite, crack open a cider—or three, now that there's no pre-kinkytimes 2-drink maximum hanging over my head—flop back onto one of Max's fancy folding chairs and just...think.

I zip and button my jeans, brush off as much dirt as I can and turn to the shadow I just had sex with. "Uh..." God, how on earth am I feeling awkward right now? I huff out a half-laugh and shake my head, which he probably can't see anyway. "Um. Are you—?"

"No talking," he whispers.

I blush, chastised. It's uncomfortable and not remotely how this evening is allowed to end. I force my voice into an unrecognizable hush. "Sorry. Thanks. Good night."

"Do you need afterca—"

"Nope!" Shit. Too loud. "No. Thank you." A forced smile, which he'll never see. "Take care, now."

With as much dignity as I can channel into my stained, bruised, and freshly fucked frame, I stumble off in what I hope is the right direction.

My stranger... Well, I have no idea what he does next. And I guess that's the point.

5

Grace

I wake up early the next morning.

Wait. Did I do it? For a few seconds, I'm not sure I actually did. Was it even real?

I test my limbs. Oh, yeah. That shoulder's bruised. Amongst other things.

I give myself a long, lazy stretch, and check in.

Am I okay, though?

It hurts, yeah. But other than that... I feel used in the best possible way. And excited, like there's something unexplored winking on the horizon.

Crap. That's not how this is supposed to go. I'm supposed to feel replete. Satisfied. Done with the fantasy. I've had the orgasm, after all. I've completed the thing, gotten it out of my system. Now, I can move on with my life. This fantasy and any relationships I might have don't even exist on the same plane.

But the *orgasm*. It was nothing like the ones I've had on my own. I mean, I know how to make myself come just fine, but feeling that close to the surface, that big and open and pulsing with pleasure from another person's touch was a different beast entirely.

Grinning to myself, I cast a glance at Max and see she's rolled up into a little ball on her bed. Better get out before I wake her up.

Outside, the air is fresh and it's absolutely quiet, aside from the bright chirping of birds. And still. The surrounding campsites and their late night scenes of bacchanal and mirth appear entirely deserted. I guess kink campers aren't exactly morning people.

I'm glad for that. After slinking back to the Thunderdome last night under cover of darkness, I didn't take the time for a drink or a shower or a moment's contemplation under the stars. I just barely cleaned myself off and made it into my PJs and plush glamping bed before passing out.

Out in our kitchen area, I put water on to boil and stretch again, luxuriating in the twinges and pains and the aches yet to come. My body's like a machine that's been taken to its limit. Used, for sure, but in the way God intended. Or something.

I sigh, giving myself an internal eyeroll.

No. No, I'm not doing embarrassment or shame or any of that other bullshit. This is one morning after

I'm going to relish as much as I can. I'm going to soak in it and relive it and do my best to remember every single second. Because it's mine. The whole experience. It's my totally guilt-free, one-off chance to get it out of my system.

And that's just what I did.

I give a passing jogger a giddy wave and reconsider making coffee myself.

Maybe I'll see if the café's open. I can use the wifi to check in on Mom. And maybe I'll look at the wall where I first spotted that ad and maybe I'll just wallow in every moment of this thing I've done, from start to finish. Just once. And, hell, maybe while I'm at it, I'll revisit the scene of the crime and look for clues. Signs of our passage, so to speak. My sex clenches at the thought.

With another smile, I grab my wallet and set off for the coffee shop, my body sore, but light.

It's not until I get inside and see Lamé behind the counter, that I realize I'm not just here to relive it. She waves hello and I wave back and what I really want to do is see if he's put up another one of those ads.

I give the wall a surreptitious look, but can't tell a thing from this distance. There are too many papers pinned and taped up; too many scrawled messages, typed ads, too many responses.

What was I even thinking? That he'd want a repeat, after specifically cutting that possibility out, from the start?

As I slink up to the bar, something a little frantic beats in my chest and, though I keep the smile on my face, part of me wishes I hadn't come.

"Soooooo," Lamé leans far forward, setting both of her elbows on the counter and, in the process opening the neckline to her diaphanous turquoise gown and flashing her lightly furred chest—the hair's dyed blue today—and a sparkly, sheer bra that reminds me of mermaids and an Ice Capades show I saw with my grandparents as a kid. Her hair's long and sleek and liquid and everything about her is like water. The way she oozes when she moves, slow and graceful and easy, the happily placid way she watches me, waiting, not forcing things. She's a bright, cheery person, on the outside, but there are depths here, I think, that not many people probably know.

Of course, all that's conjecture. An impression. But then the urge to draw her takes me by surprise. It's more like an itch than getting bopped on the head, but itches, I think, will get to you when shock and awe fails. For years, all creativity's left me. I paint houses for a living, not canvases, and suddenly, my second morning at Camp Haven, the day after I've let myself live my deepest fantasy, I want to pick up a stick of charcoal and see just how fluid this woman would look on the page.

"Whoa. That bad, huh?"

Confused, I meet her gaze. "What?"

"Last night. Your, uh, encounter."

Without meaning to, I give the message wall another glance and then turn back to her smiling face and I swear she knows everything going on in my brain right now. She confirms this when she leans closer, lowers her head to my ear and says, "I knew it. It was good, right? Like the best sex you've ever had?"

Just the mention of it brings everything back to me in an overwhelming wave. The way his big hand cupped my neck, the warm, even cadence of his breath—until things got wild and he lost that controlled edge and—

I can't breathe for a second. A few seconds actually. Finally, I get my act together and turn, finding myself way too close to Lamé's knowing gaze, her smiling mouth. I should tell her it was fun and grab a coffee and just go, but I want something, I guess. I haven't figured out what it is yet, but it's there, glimmering just out of reach.

"It was..." I swallow, trying to pinpoint one feeling, one word that I can share with this near-stranger. "Transformative."

"Whoa. That's a big-ass word right there." She moves away—finally—and sets to work making a coffee. I imagine it's mine, since there's no one else here, but it seems unlikely she'd remember my order from yesterday, considering the number of drinks she probably makes in a day.

I pull out my phone and type a quick message to Mom.

Me: *How is everything?*

Of course she replies within seconds. She's probably up and doing her first online Sudoku of the day right now. Though she can barely hold a pen anymore, she's an ace with her phone. Thank God for talk to text.

Mom: *Aren't you supposed to be on vacation right now?*

The vacation part she knows about. Just not what kind of vacation this is, which is definitely a source of guilt.

Me: *Just checking in.*

Mom: *All is well, Gracie. I'm on second tea, Vanessa's hovering. Put your phone away and enjoy yourself, FFS.* After a second: *And send me pictures!*

Yeah, right.

Me: *Okay. Love you.*

Mom: *Don't forget to flirt! Get out there, Rosebud!*

If only she knew.

Mom, who never for a second wanted me to give up my dreams in order to take care of her, was ecstatic when she found out Max had convinced me to take time off.

"I'm not surprised, though," Lamé says over her shoulder, shimmying when the music changes and an old Massive Attack song comes on.

"Surprised?" I have no idea what she's talking about.

"About the transformative thing."

Am I surprised? I don't know. I can't tell. What I feel right now is like I've been blown wide open.

I want to know who he was, this man who threw my body so deeply into pleasure. I wish I could ask Lamé, though that's clearly against the rules.

Tell me more, I want to say. Who is he? What's his name? Or just a vague description will do. Something to wank over. What color's his hair? Is it short? How the hell do I not even know that? I wish he hadn't worn the ski mask, so I could have reached back and felt his hair, run my fingers through it to know at least the texture. Did he have facial hair? I want to know it all. It seems unfair that he's pulled my hair and felt the details of my body and I've got nothing but his overall mass to work with.

His eyes are what I wish I'd seen the most. I mean, his body would have been good masturbation fodder at least, but his eyes... Are they dark, like mine? Or bright? Are they as intense as...well, him? What if he's not intense at all in real life? He could be like a bank teller or something, right? Just plugging numbers in and depositing checks by day, all smiley and easy going, and at night...

"Ooooooh!" She points at the tattoo that snakes down from the sleeve of my T-shirt to disappear at my wrist. "Savage," she breathes. "And here's your latte. Anything else?"

"Could I have one for Max, please? With lots of that vanilla syrup stuff. I'm impressed you remember mine."

"You got it, hon." Lamé's expression loses its evil twinkle. She leans toward me again, looking almost sad. "I'm glad it was good. But don't look for him again, okay? He's..." She blinks, as if she's got something in her eyes. "Complicated. Here. Coffees are on the house."

"Yeah. No. Once is good. Once is all I want." I thank her, shove a tip in her jar, and start to leave, then stop, already regretting what I'm about to say. "I hope he had a good time, too, you know?"

She makes a *What?* face. "Oh, honey. I'm sure he did."

"Okay, good. Because for me, it was amazing. It was..." Like finally figuring out what makes me tick. Well, at least part of me. The deep down dirty bits. "Liberating. And it was definitely a one-off. I just came here to get it out of my system, then go home. Now, I'm done. I can move on."

"Mm hm." Looking highly skeptical, she goes on. "You know that's not how it works, right?"

I suspect she's right, given how I feel inside right now. Like a tap inside me's opened when I'd hoped to shut it tight. "Yeah," I concede, though it's hard admitting it to myself.

"Good. The worst thing you can do is try to repress stuff like this. It's who you are." Her eyes go wide as they focus behind me. "Morning, boss." I turn to see a guy who's as out of place at Camp Haven as I am. We're both wearing worn T-shirts and jeans, for one thing—definitely not the typical uniform.

Everyone I've seen here is primped and waxed and dyed and either close to naked or absolutely dressed to the nines and beyond. This guy, though, has messy hair that's so dusty, I can't make out the color. His T-shirt's threadbare in places, his hands stained, his boots more suited to a work site than a sex camp.

He nods in reply to Lamé's greeting and gives me a cursory glance before walking up to grab the steaming coffee she's already placed on the counter.

"Boss." He's got his face in his cup when she starts talking. "I want you to meet—"

His hand goes up to stop her.

Lamé rolls her eyes and shrugs my way, with a big, theatrical sigh. "Anyway, honey. I'm glad you're feeling good after what you did last night." She winks and waves goodbye, grabs a towel and wipes at the counter. I guess this conversation is done.

I'm close to the door when she says something that almost makes me stumble. "We all deserve a chance at happiness. Right, boss?"

I don't stick around to hear the dude's grumbled answer. I've got a late-night assignation to rehash in my head.

6

Grace

Camp Haven's an easy place to get distracted. It's an easy place to lose yourself or, hell, I guess find yourself for some of us. My first day here was nothing but distractions. I mean, the first thing I saw after passing through the camp's imposing front gate was a naked, muscular male ass, framed by chaps and cowboy boots, traipsing down the gravel drive.

And that was before check-in.

I got lost in the ambiance that first day, surprised at how sunny and happy everybody seemed, despite the whips and collars and outdoor sex. Or maybe because of it. I've honestly never seen such a carefree group, ready for pleasure, open to anything, non-judgmental, communicative.

It's good. Beautiful, actually.

Too bad I don't notice any of that right now. The minute I leave the coffee shop, I'm lost in my head, barely aware of the woman who greets me as she leads her yawning human pet to grab a morning drink from Lamé.

As I walk past the pool toward the little village of campsites, where people are just starting to emerge, my mind's completely lost in the dark of last night. The rich aroma of coffee wafting from my cup brings back the earthy scent of dirt and bark, mixed with my predator's smell—the one I'll never be able to describe. God, it was good. Skin, heat, sex.

I'm nearly panting by the time I arrive at the Thunderdome, where Max is just emerging from our big, fancy tent. Her hair's poking out in all directions, her eyes at half-mast behind her glasses. She's wearing a tank top and men's boxers, her face sleep-lined and soft, and I'm so full of affection that I just want to hug her.

I'm not much of a hugger, though, so I smile and wave, laughing at the comical double-take she gives me. "What?"

"Did you just go back into the woods and do it all over again?"

My insides clench up at the thought. "No." Why do I sound almost guilty?

"You look all dreamy-eyed." She wipes a smudge off my neck. "And filthy."

I want to go back. Not just to revisit the scene like I intend, but to repeat the entire adventure. With my stranger. And that's not part of the plan.

One and done. That was it. For him, obviously, but for me, too, despite what Lamé said. I don't need complications in my life. I've got responsibilities and getting hunted down and fucked on the regular doesn't fit in anywhere. At all.

"It was a one-time thing. You know that." I throw Max a look and hand her Lamé's special coffee.

"Oh, bless you, Rosebud."

I roll my eyes at the old nickname. Dad gave it to me when I was a kid. Mom still uses it sometimes, but mostly it's just Max when she's condescending.

"And *bless* you, Father, for I have sinned."

I snort. "I'll bet."

I turn and watch a pale-haired white man crawl by, a tiny Black woman who's probably someone's grandma sitting astride him, smacking his fleshy flank with a riding crop. He's entirely naked, while she's wearing some kind of beauty queen gown, or maybe a prom dress, sequins, tiara, long gloves, and all. She turns to give us a regal smile with a cupped-handed parade wave. We wave back. It's eight in the fucking morning.

Max takes a long, luxurious pull at her coffee that makes me wish I was working on my first sip, too, and sinks into a lawn chair. "Oh, yeah. I sinned last night in the Dungeon. You remember Halo and Flow?"

"Those two massive guys with all the tattoos?"

She nods. "And Micah?"

I squint, trying to recall one face from the hundreds she's introduced me to in the past two days. Max—or Mad Max as she's known here—is quite popular.

"The Black guy in silver nut huggers at dinner last night. He was with Mistress Tan and..."

"Oh my God, right." I remember the man in question. He was beautiful, his face crushingly sweet and handsome, with soft brown eyes and plush lips, his body like something you'd see in the Louvre, though significantly larger in the package region. I know this because I saw it uncovered later, in bright, shining technicolor, bare but for a brutal line of piercings. I didn't stick around the Dungeon long enough to see him use the thing.

"He's *such* a sadist." She sighs with a grin and leans back to lift her tank and show me the fresh bruises on her rib cage.

"Jesus, dude." It's not easy for me to suppress a shudder, but I do. Max doesn't like how upset I get and I honestly can't relate to the getting beaten for fun thing but, hell, most people outside of these walls likely wouldn't understand what I did last night, so I keep my reservations to myself.

Now that I think about it, it hasn't bothered me to watch the floggings and whippings and diverse beatings happening in the Dungeon every evening. It's the consequences that I have trouble with. Or maybe it's just seeing the visible aftermath on my friend's skin.

"Nice, right?"

I force a smile to my face and hide behind a gulp of too-hot coffee.

Thankfully, we sink into silence, both of us probably rehashing last night's festivities. I'm pretty sure I'm the only one who feels any guilt about what I did.

No, it's not entirely guilt. It's...regret isn't the word, because I definitely don't regret it. Two consenting adults getting their rocks off in unconventional ways isn't something I'll ever see in a negative light. I might have once upon a time, but Max has used logic and her very convincing therapy speak to clean that right out of me.

So, what's wrong? Why do I feel off-kilter like this?

"You still set on the one-time to get it out of your system thing?" she asks lightly. "Or is there a chance you'll go back in for seconds?"

"He said no repeats," I reply without thinking.

"Right. Yep. He sure did." She's using that gentle, but straightforward voice again, the no-nonsense voice she's always used to show me reason. It's probably the way she talks to her therapy clients and it brooks no argument. Honestly, though, I don't have much argument in me.

"You're gonna make me say it, aren't you, Max?"

"Mm mm." Her shoulders do a slow side-to-side sway in her chair. It's not a victory dance, exactly, but there's a definite undercurrent of *I told you so*.

"I don't want to have to smack you on that stupid bruise," I say with grudging humor.

Her cackle's high and delighted. It's one of my favorite sounds, even when I'm the brunt of it. *Especially* then.

When she tilts her head and sets it on my shoulder, there's nothing but love between us.

"Yeah, dammit." I sigh, letting my head sink onto hers. "I want to do it again."

"You could go put up an ad of your own."

I could, couldn't I?

Feeling brighter, I plant a loud kiss on the crown of her head and stand up. "I think I will."

7

Liev

I'M out in my studio, high up on the scaffolding, forcing myself to concentrate on what I'm doing, when my phone buzzes in my pocket. I've got a chisel in one hand, a hammer in the other and a half-ton of granite between my legs.

I ignore the sound. Probably a pocket call. The Camp Haven staff knows better than to use my number. It's in the rule book, front and center.

Emergency number. Use only in case of:
Something to fix.
Someone to patch up.
Some asshole to kick off the premises.

They also know that, in case of a true emergency,

calling once isn't enough, so when the buzzing starts up again, I figure it's one of the sanctioned reasons and pick up. "Better be good."

"Need you down here stat, Boss!" Kris Koski, aka Lamé, replies, not nearly frantic enough to be making this kind of call.

"What is it?" With the phone tucked between my ear and my shoulder, I'm already halfway down the scaffold.

"Coffee machine's on the fritz. Just won't work. There's a line out the door and you know how the morning crowd is, right? It'll be *Lord of the Flies* here soon. I know you're working and it's a bad time, but..."

I half listen as Kris lists all the reasons this is a national emergency. The fact is, I don't much care if people get their morning coffee or not. It's not life or death, unlike some of the calls I've gotten, like last year, when I had to climb a tree to cut a woman out of some asshole's sub-par rope work. Then, of course, I had to throw her play partner out for general idiocy.

I grab my tool box and let Lamé go on, more because I know they've got an audience down there than for my own sake, push through my front gate, taking the time to latch it behind me, and head off for the coffee shop at a jog. After a minute, Lamé stops long enough for me to mention I'm on my way, says a rushed, "*Okaybye*," and hangs up.

By the time I get there, the crowd's overflowing practically to the pool. I'm used to their stares and ignore them, along with their not-so-subtly whispered mentions of the Overlord, as I walk by.

Yes, they call me the Overlord. Yes, I know this. No, I don't give a shit. They can call me whatever the hell they want. Overlord makes a funny kind of sense, if you consider that the camp is mine and I watch over it from my house up on the hill, only stepping in when something goes wrong. It's not a name I'd have chosen and wasn't the name I used back when I was an active part of the scene, but it's stuck.

I ignore it.

"Oh, my God. Oh my God. Thank God you're here, I've tried everything. Absolutely everything. Turned it off. On again. Flipped those little switchies on the back." Lamé goes on, listing every possible thing they could have done to fix the fickle, old machine.

Tuning them out, I head around the counter and set down my tools. I have to admit, at least to myself, that I'm happy for the distraction. Work wasn't doing it for me today. Maybe if I were in the early stages, cutting out big chunks of rock to uncover the sculpture's more general shapes, I'd have been able to lose myself in it, but this late stage finishing isn't all that exciting, which means my mind's been wandering.

Right back to last night.

Shit, even now, here, with a perfectly good problem to solve, Lamé's lamenting, and a couple dozen observers thrown in as added distraction, I can picture it perfectly.

My pulse kicks up, my dick goes half-hard, and every muscle tenses with the memory of her arms and legs and fingers tearing at me, her ragged breathing blowing life into my lungs.

It was a fluke, how good it was, but it felt so fucking real. So right. I can't pinpoint one thing that made her different from all the others.

But it's there.

"Line's blocked," I say over my shoulder. "You flush it?"

"Oh, of course, Boss. Yeah. Yep. Flushed it, washed it…"

I expect a third line from Lamé, who likes rhythm. When nothing comes, I look up, then narrow my eyes at their expression. Instantly, my hackles are up, the way they were when I walked into the house the one time Helen set up a surprise party for my birthday.

My arms drop to my sides. "What's going on?"

Lamé's eyes widen innocently, just compounding the whole sensation. "What? Nothing."

I give them a long, narrow look and then follow the line back to the source of the problem. While my hands work, I ignore the disquiet and let myself remember.

Last night was like dancing or something. The way I imagine a really good pair of dancers feel when they come together. The moves felt choreographed, although not rehearsed, which makes no fucking sense, except in my brain. Every time I moved, she responded and every response was straight from my playbook.

Then there was the mystery woman's voice.

All the blood in my body goes to my dick.

I sigh and shut my eyes, just for a second.

"You okay, Boss?" Of course Lamé notices. We've known each other too long and too well for any change in my behavior to get past them. Shit, I knew Lamé as a teen who came to the local Kink and Fetish group for help and wound up talking to me. There's been so much pain in their life. So much misunderstanding, so much hatred from family, peers, even professionals who should have known better.

Kris was one of the reasons Helen and I bought this old scout camp and turned it into what it is now: a safe place.

Above all, though, Kris is quite possibly one of the only reasons I'm alive today. Not possibly. Definitely. I wouldn't be here if it weren't for her and Zion—the two people I count as close friends.

So, basically, Kris will continue to annoy me, but they can do no wrong. Lifetime pass.

"Oh. There! You got it! Moby Dick will live another day!" Kris—Lamé—claps their hands and jumps up and down, although how that's possible on roller skates I'll never understand.

"You'll put your eye out in those things," I tell them, for the seven millionth time.

"You old fogey," they say, throwing one arm around me in a quick side hug, which I brush off, to no one's surprise. Their affection is immediately transferred to the big, ancient espresso machine known as Moby Dick. It's been painted light blue in places, to emulate the famous sea creature, although clearly we're all ignoring that whole chapter on the whiteness of the whale. "You're the best. You're magic. A magician! You're the bees' knees and the cat's pajamas and—"

Together, we finish their sentence. "Everything good in the world."

Lamé giggles and I offer up a look that's not a frown. I'm halfway around the counter, heading toward the exit when they let out a light shriek. "Oh my God, it's sprayed me!"

"You okay?" I drop my toolbox and turn back.

"I'm fine. I mean, my dress isn't, but... Could you just..." Lamé throws their arms up in the air, looking helpless. "Could you grab me a couple extra bar towels from storage? I seem to have run out. I don't know *how* I did that."

Without hesitating, I walk to the door to the back —where all the messages are posted. Someone shouts something about a wet T-shirt contest. Lamé giggles. From the speakers, Beyoncé sings about putting a ring on it and there, right where I posted my ad, smack in the middle of the message board, there's another, written on the same yellow card stock, the writing in thick block letters, just like mine. It's a replica in every way. Except for the words.

I want a repeat.

I'll be there again tonight.

That's it. That's all it says.

I stand there and stare, feeling as if I've slipped into another time, another dimension. I'm here now, while the rest of the room, the whole world, is still back there, doing what they were doing a minute ago.

I specifically said no repeats.

My vision goes hazy.

I could taste her. Force her legs wide and eat her cunt until she screams and then I could cover her mouth with my hand and make her take it in silence. I'd bite her there. And higher. Her chest, her neck. I want to leave a mark.

Fuck. My cock's hard as nails.

Someone whoops, bursting my invisible bubble, and I can't believe it's still Beyoncé singing. Still the same crowd, the same day. I shake my head, shove open the door and head inside, only remembering what I've come for after staring at a wall for a few seconds. Fighting the urge to lock myself into the little office and jerk off, I grab the towels and return to the chaos of morning at the Camp Haven Coffee Shop.

I put the towels on the bar, nod at Lamé's wide-eyed thank you, and get the hell out of there as fast as I can.

About halfway home I come to an abrupt stop. "Sonofabitch."

That was a set up. How did I not see what Lamé was doing? They know that espresso machine better than anyone. They know where to kick when it gets cranky, how to coddle it back to life. Hell, Lamé could fix the damn thing blindfolded. I know them way too well to let them snow me like that.

Or not. At least not as distracted as I've been today.

Feeling like an idiot, I take out my phone and call them.

"Camp Haven," they answer. "You can leave, but you better come first."

I snort, surprising myself. "Alright, Kris. You had your fun. Now take it down."

"What?" There's a noisy pause when I can just picture them removing the phone from their face to stare at it as if they just can't believe their ears. A second later, they're back. "Who is this?"

"You know who it is. Quit your theatrics and listen."

"That you, Boss? It sounds like you, but it can't be. The words are all wrong."

"Did you put that ad up?"

"Nope."

My belly clenches hard with excitement. "Okay." With a long-suffering sigh I give in. "You were right, Kris. This one is..."

"Say it. Go on. Say it."

"It was different."

"No, not it."

"Jesus. Okay. Fine. She. The woman. The one from last night. She was different."

Kris grumps a little. "I believe the word I used was *special*. She's special and she's also just what Doctor Lamé ordered for you." Something rustles and they yell out, "Skinny half-caff for Daddy Larry!"

"I need you to take the note down."

"Sure, hon. Hey Lar, baby!" they yell. "Would you be an angel and grab that little piece of paper off the board for me? The yellow one. Fabulous. Thank you, you're such a doll."

"Does Daddy Larry know who you're on the phone with? For fuck's sake, Kris, if he puts two and—"

"Why? Want me to invite him, too? I could. His Little's a real cutie. About twice his age, but since Larry's just this side of legal, that's not—"

I'm tempted to hang up, but I've reached the ripe old age of thirty-three without ever doing so and I don't plan to start now. Instead, I interrupt. "I didn't say I'd meet her tonight. I just need you to take it off the board. I'm not going, but we can't have—"

"Oh, honey, you'll be there. You almost cracked a smile this morning. First time in three years I've seen anything other than a scowl on that pretty mug of yours. Now go on and get all gussied up so you can grab another dose of that magic pussy. I'll bet it goes great with that big, fat, magic pen—"

"Please stop talking."

"Fine." Lamé blows a raspberry and ends the call.

At least one of us got to hang up.

8

Grace

TONIGHT'S DIFFERENT. Already, when I get dressed, it's not for some amorphous idea of a thing that I'm into, but for him: The man whose smell I know, whose rough hands I felt. The man who gave me my first ever partnered orgasm and left every other sexual experience in the dust.

The man whose arms held me together while he flayed me wide open.

For him, I put on my favorite T-shirt. It's got the tiniest bit of lace at both shoulders. That's a lot of embellishment for me. He'll never see it and probably won't know the difference, but I will. I'll know it's fancier than anything I own except for the prom dress at the back of my closet.

Before pulling on the shirt, I waste a few minutes debating the usefulness of a bra, recall the way he yanked almost angrily at the cups, and decide to keep it. I liked being pried apart, one piece at a time. I liked everything that happened. If I could do anything different tonight, it would be to draw out every single beat, make it all last longer.

That's why I don't accept the skirt Max tries to give me. "No thanks," I tell her. "I'm good with shorts.

"But, Gracie!" She shakes the black cotton in my face. It's kind of hilarious to watch the sexy night version of her Camp Haven self—Mad Max—acting like the regular Max I've always known. Like, we could be twelve again and arguing over boys and what show we're going to watch, except she's wearing fishnets and a short corset that shows off her tattoos and bruises and…shit, those pinpricks have got to be from needle play, which I didn't even realize she was into. She's still wearing the thick-heeled, steel-toed boots her camp persona prefers and the little backpack, filled with water and first-aid supplies and scissors and condoms and a few pairs of those flexible cuffs for lord knows what reason, but she's also sporting bright red lips and dark smokey eyes and thick fake lashes.

"A skirt's easy access," she whines. "You need easy access."

I just shrug, feeling the tiniest little thread of self-satisfaction and...ownership, I guess you'd call it. This is *my* kink, not hers. It's a rarity for me to be into something that doesn't particularly turn Max on.

She's pansexual and polyamorous and kinky as hell and up for most everything. I'm sure, for example, that she'd be fine with having a person hunt her down and fuck her. She'd have no issue with it. It's not, however, what lights her up inside.

Whereas I'm getting wound up again just remembering the way he worked to get my pants off, the way they trapped my legs together, binding me until he yanked one leg all the way off, with a quiet, satisfied grunt.

"I like that it's not easy to get to me."

"Hmmmmmm." Her gaze focuses on me, bright and curious behind her cat-eye glasses. "Interesting."

"How so?"

"Would you say that the first-ever-orgasm-with-a-partner thing was the best part for you, or was it something else? I mean, if you had to isolate last night to one single shining moment. What would it be?"

I pause halfway through pulling my shorts up under my robe. As far as I can tell, I'm the only person here who gives a crap if people see me naked...or even in my underwear. It's ironic, now that I think about what I did outside last night. Then again, it was dark. Nobody there to see me.

The darkness had definite appeal—the

anonymity, but also the way it made me forget myself.

I do want to see him, though. I'd brave the light for that alone. We won't have any tonight, either, but I'd give a hell of a lot to see just one of my stranger's expressions.

Did he look angry when he fisted my hair and pulled? Stern? Does he have a boyish face that doesn't go at all with the rest of him? Maybe he can't stand the idea of anyone not taking that sweet, young face seriously? Is he ugly? I wouldn't mind that. At all. Maybe a scar or two. A big nose, a permanent grimace.

Max, who's now standing there just staring at me, arms crossed, clears her throat.

I button my shorts, giving her a dull look, and suddenly remember that she asked me a question. Oh, right. What was the best moment?

Was it when he bit me? God, it doesn't feel real right now. Or the second he came after me in the dark, like the very first moment I felt his presence. But then I remember how my body jumped when he gripped my pubic hair, hard, and everything sort of melts inside, from my chest to my pelvis. He took something I've always felt a little weird about—the fact that so many women today shave off all their hair—and flipped it right over. I'm glad I have hair for him to grab. It's like the bra. Like the panties and the buttons on my shorts. They're all just obstacles. Maybe the obstacles are as satisfying as the goal.

Huh.

I look at Max, suddenly serious. "Every single thing that happened was the best of that thing. Every bit of it was... I want to say good, but that's not it. It wasn't good, it was, like..." I'm not the best at expressing my inner self to others, but I want to find this word. I need it. "I was shook."

Max snorts. "Shook, huh? You're using that word now?"

"Maybe." I grab the bright red lipstick she's just put on and dab the slightest bit on my bottom lip, then look in her hand mirror and rub it entirely off. "I'm shaken. Definitely stirred. Also kind of crushed. Melted." I consider. "A lot of ice things."

"Except frozen, I hope." She turns and eyes me up and down, puts her hand out for the lipstick and when I return it, leans in and carefully slides it over all of my mouth. And not the tint I was looking for, but a full on layer. Doing my own lipstick makes me look like a clown, but when I glance in the mirror, I don't hate it. I picture him smearing it with his fingers, his mouth. Suddenly, it's hard to breathe.

"You're so gorgeous." Max steps up and wraps her arms around me from behind. It's not easy, given that I've got almost a foot on her. "When are you gonna do my tattoo?"

"When I can get the equipment." One day. When I've paid off all the medical debt and managed to find a bigger place for me and Mom. Then I'll think about my tattoo shop.

"I'm so glad you're doing this, Grace. You've been so..."

I tense up. I can't help it.

"So lost, I think, with men and love and everything." I start to turn and she stops me. "I'm not saying this will solve all your problems or anything like that, but it's good that you're exploring. Finally." Another quick squeeze. "This is you. The real you. Not the you who takes care of your mom every night or the you who yells at the debt collectors, or the version who talks to clients or those bozos you work with. This is like... You're like the one I went to school with. The Gracie who drew pictures of everything. Everywhere. All the time. The Gracie whose hands got scratched up from making beautiful art out of trash. The Gracie who slapped Ben Fulton across the face for calling me the B word when we were ten and the Gracie who was there that night it all went to hell senior year." I feel her shrug against my back before her hold loosens. It's funny how my stranger held me together with his arms and now Max has done the same and she's let me go and I can only stand here awkwardly while she plows a hole in my heart.

"I like this Gracie. I love her." She zips the lipstick into her backpack and sucks in a deep, audible breath. "I wish you loved her as much as I do."

My mouth is open, though I've got no idea what to say after that speech. It swallowed me up and spat me out and made me feel loved and seen and also sad for the life I once dreamed of. It's funny, because of the two of us, growing up, Max definitely had it harder, and yet she's always been truer to herself. She's always known who she was, whereas I let life pry me away from who I wanted to be.

"Come on." She grabs a couple condoms from her bag, slips them into my pocket, then threads her arm through mine, tugging me forward. "I'll walk you to your mauling."

If he shows up, of course.

9

Liev

I'M RUNNING LATE. It's especially annoying, given that I hadn't planned on meeting her at all tonight.

I tried not to.

But I knew, just as Lamé predicted, that I'd show up in the end. Then a golf cart broke down and an older camper had a nasty fall, which thankfully our on-site medical staff was able to help with. I headed back up to the house for a clean shirt and it was nearing time to be there. Now I'm racing down the path in the dark.

I should slow down, but I can't stand the idea of leaving my mystery woman waiting there, alone. Maybe leaving before I arrive.

I nod at the person working security, glad to see them here.

When I get to the spot, I'm breathing too hard to be the calm, cool hunter I prefer, but it's too late. I hear her, walking through the woods, slightly south of where we were last night.

Immediately, my hackles—or whatever the human equivalent is—rise and everything sharpens. My vision, my hearing, my sense of smell. Even my skin feels more sensitive, picking up on things I'd never usually notice. Calm flows through me, like oxygen in my veins. Like a drug.

It's always been this way, since the first time I chased a woman. That first time was...

I blow out a slow, relaxing breath and push back that well-worn memory. First times are always special and that one doubly so—me and Helen, me and my inner beast. Hell, me and myself. I was barely an adult going into that night, but I left fully me, subtly different, wiser, more deeply connected with who I was meant to be.

She—or her silhouette—shifts away from a group of trees to my left. Rather than give chase, I pull on my mask, wait, and listen, head tilted, breathing as quiet as I can get it. Just watch. I like the way she moves, her steps careful, but not overly cautious. Other things come back now that I'm here—now that I'm allowing them to. Her height was good. Different. And she was strong. That was a very pleasant surprise.

I reach down and press a palm to my cock. It's heavy and warm, like the sultry summer air. It was oppressive today. Absolutely sweltering. Now, though, I welcome the heat. It's a blanket around us. Another presence.

I move now, let my footsteps get as loud as they want, carelessly sending rocks careening off the path into the underbrush. I want her to call out again, like she did last night. It switched a flip, brought my inner predator closer to the surface than it's been in ages.

I scuff noisily to a stop and will her to say something, cracking my knuckles slowly, loudly. There's no denying the threat now.

"Um. Hello?" The rules say she shouldn't talk, but fuck me, her voice. That rough little edge, so raspy and raw. "Are you..." She gives me a low, nervous laugh. "Is someone there? Here? Are you here?"

I clear my throat, just to taunt her.

She gasps. "Oh, God. Look, could you..." Her silhouette shuffles back a couple steps. "Listen. I just need to get home. Okay? Please?"

A dark, evil sound rumbles from my chest. It's not quite a laugh, but it's not far. I want to reply, but it's best not to. Whispers only. That's my rule. Although I love that she's not following it. Like her body, like the way she runs and fights, like the tight clasp of her cunt, her voice plucks at some echoing chord inside me.

I inhale the scent of pine and rotting leaves. She

spins and sprints. I take off behind her, my steps even and sure. My terrain. My land. My woman.

And maybe that last bit's not true in the real world, but my inner Primal doesn't give a shit. As far as the beast is concerned, she's his. Mine.

The way the tension's strung between us, she can run all she wants, I could catch her with my eyes shut. I close them for a second and follow the pull.

She thrashes into a denser area, making her way toward the clearing. I pick up the pace, narrow the distance, let sense-memory lead, and then I'm on her. I tackle her this time, torquing before we hit to take the brunt of the fall. It's like my football-playing days, except my dick was never hard as nails back then. Well, that and I never fucked any of my opponents.

She's halfway up before I drag her back down, adrenaline coursing through me so fast I barely soften my hold. She fights me harder tonight, forcing me to do the same. With every corkscrew of her body, every shallow kick, every elbow to my side, the boundaries shift closer to realism and deeper into my wheelhouse.

We're a grunting, writhing mass, groping in the dark, by the time I've got her completely pinned.

"I should push your face into the dirt and fuck you right now," I whisper straight into her ear.

Moaning, she trembles harder.

Jesus, I've never had someone whose reactions were so in sync with mine. It's like she pulled the playbook from my brain and brought it into full, living color right here, under the stars.

"But I won't," I warn, knowing that my girl won't like it.

She thrashes, as I expected, and goddamn, she's strong. Our bodies roll fast and hard. What is this? Fucking Jiu Jitsu? I've probably got seventy-five pounds on her, but she's not letting up. Every second the tussle drags on, I get hotter, harder, less controlled.

Finally, I get an opening, get her on her back, press my aching dick to the hot place between her legs. She tries to haul herself to one side, I wind a hand in her hair. She freezes.

"Don't you fucking move again."

I'm already working at her shorts when she replies. "Or what?"

Grace

I have no idea what kind of threat to expect. Honestly, I'm not thinking too straight by this point. I'm on fire.

It's unreasonable. It's probably dangerous. It's also the most unbelievably exciting moment of my life. Not just sexual moment. I mean *any* moment. If

I could take the way his fist feels in my hair and make it last forever, I would.

The last thing I expect when I thrash this time is for him to slap his hand on my pussy and grip the crotch of my shorts, using it to hold me in place, like a handle.

"Told you not to move," he says, his voice nothing but a rasp in the night, though it's as solidly threatening as the earth beneath my bruised ass.

Shit. Shit, what's he going to do? Everything my brain comes up with—another slap between my legs, pinching my breasts, making me take him in my mouth—sends my libido rocketing higher, harder. I'm so turned on right now, I'm not sure it would take more than a couple quick swats like that to make me climax.

"What?" I gasp when he slowly twists the crotch of my shorts. "What are you gonna do?"

"I'd spank you..."

Oh God, yes. Please. Please spank me. Lay me over your knee and—

"But you'd like it too much."

How does he know that? For the first time, something like fear crawls up my spine.

"Oh God," I mutter aloud.

Another hard torque of my shorts sends air rushing against my sex, harsh and cold against my wet heat. The move's crude, designed to hurt, maybe frighten, while it opens me up to the elements.

And I've still got the damn shorts on.

"You don't come."

I groan. "No. Please, that's the one th—"

He slaps my half-bared pussy, stopping me mid-word. My body tries to curl up, but he's stretching me out tight as a string. "I've never…"

Another slap sends my mind spiraling somewhere into the trees, not quite coming, but close. The fist tightens in my hair, his body shifts. "You've never what?" His whisper's harsh and weird, like he's more out of breath than I realized. Like I'm not the only one losing it here.

I hesitate, embarrassed for the first time since this thing started.

Another slap to my pussy makes me groan. "What?" he urges, so pissed off I'm almost scared.

At the same time, I want him to grind his palm against my clit, I want pressure. I want his cock.

I want to wrap my hands in his hair, too. Is it short? I think it's short, but it's impossible to tell with the mask. I want to feel how rough his cheeks are, let my hands circle his throat to gauge its girth, the way his Adam's apple moves. He feels big—all of him. Heavy, strong, wide as a goddamn wall.

And I want to see the big cock that stretched me open last night, weigh it in my hand, taste it.

Instead, I hold still and force myself to answer. "I never orgasmed with a partner. Before last night." And then, because this part seems important. "Before *you*."

He doesn't respond right away, though I sense a

change. Of course, that could always be my imagination. It's had a lot of practice, after all.

"From penetration?"

"From anything. You're my first." He jerks, as if startled and I correct myself. "Doing this, I mean. Not...not sex."

"Okay."

A laugh rasps out from my lungs, low and broken apart, the way my voice always is when things get intense.

Slowly, while we whisper back and forth, his fingers slip past my shorts and the underwear he's twisted into a rope, to spread me wide. It's a slow, languid exploration and not at all what we've done thus far. It doesn't feel wrong—far from it—but it's different and I have the feeling it's not what he's here for.

I mean, none of this is exactly setting the scene for intimacy, physical or otherwise.

And yet... One thick knuckle glides easily between my lips, the sound so loud it's sinful.

"You're soaked," he rasps, moving lower, as if to watch fingers that he can't possibly see.

At some point, he let go of my hair. I have no idea when. I'm so focused on what he's doing between my legs, the rest of me might as well not exist. Another slide, the sound obscene, the feeling...luxurious. Oh, oh, and then the rough edge of his skin against my clit —too much. It's too much. I arch and strain to curl up and he shifts his heavy weight so I'm pinned to the ground, his face right there, his breath heating my core.

With a low curse, he gets my shorts open, works them down my thighs, reminding me to breathe deep and live in this moment, and then—oh God, I'll never forget this—he rips off his mask with an irritated sound and bites my inner thigh.

I can't hold back a scream.

A big hand lands on my belly, nailing me in place. He shushes me, which is infuriating and demeaning and also tender and I'm liquid when he plays me with his breath against my skin. His teeth scrape my thigh as he breathes against me. Inhalations, deep and sensuous, followed by exhaled wafts of warm air, heavenly and earthy and so undeniably carnal and I'm nothing but skin and flesh, blood and bone, and pure, pure want.

I don't tell my hips to move or my voice to hum, they just do it. A dance and song of sheer instinct. When his mouth brushes my pussy, the pleasure's unfettered by anything conscious or worried. He licks me up and down, his hands holding me still, like a meal. Like prey that's been hunted and taken down to be enjoyed as it should be—with satisfaction.

A long lick, a slow suck. He's tasting my sex, not for me, but for *him*. With a growl, he pushes my shorts down and off entirely, my panties lost somewhere in the mix. I don't care if I never see them again. I want his mouth back on me, that tongue tasting and consuming.

"More," I demand and, rather than do things my way, he rolls me onto my belly, forces my head down in a repeat of my position last night, and lifts my ass up high.

I make a sound, half protest, half needy whine, but I don't think he hears me. Now that he's bested me in the physical fight, he'll do with me as he wishes and, holy shit, that makes my pussy clench, empty and aching with a deep, dirty kind of want. Another low shush from him sends a strain of irritation racing through me, but even that's a perfect part of this heady cocktail. Something to dissect and reexamine later with my hand, mind, and memory.

I squirm when he moves behind me and go still when his breath returns to tease me between the cheeks.

He pulls them apart. Oh God. Nobody's done this before. And certainly not the way he's moving in, all deep, hungry snarling and raspy breaths, leading with his teeth and his nose and finally, finally, his tongue.

10

Liev

Her taste is a fucking drug. Musky/salty/sweet. Exactly the flavor I've been craving. It's not just that I haven't eaten pussy in forever, it's chemistry or genetics or some unexplainable predilection for this specific combination of tastes and smells and sensations. She's got a ripe ass, soft and strong and probably too easy to bruise. I want to bruise it like a peach, though that's never once been my kink.

I dig my fingers tighter into her flesh and dive in, face first, licking up and down, from her cunt to her tight little asshole and back. I want to fuck her both places, want to absolutely consume her. The need's unrelenting, the hunger so deep I can't imagine being able to slake it tonight.

Something like fear skitters up my spine. I shove it back and let feral sounds tear from my chest and soar into the night. Christ, it feels good to be…alive.

I lick into her sweet pussy, then strain forward to suck at that swollen little clit. It sets her off, makes her shake and writhe. This dance is all the things I've been missing. I lift her up, flip and roll under, then drag her down hard so she's sitting on my face. I want to smother in her, slake the thirst and pound out all the emotion I'm dragging around.

She struggles and we roll, butting up against a tree, then back in the other direction. I'm consuming her, biting at those lips, spearing my tongue into her hot little hole, sucking hard.

I suspect she's close to coming. I know I am, but my cock needs more friction to get there. I roll her onto her back, wishing I could see the brown or pink of her skin here, the delicate whorls of hair and plump curves of flesh. I want to know the color of these curls I ache to drag her around by.

Feeling so fucking *much*, I lift her and lick from her asshole back up again, letting myself imagine how tight she'd be there, how good that would feel. Craving penetration, I lean back to work a finger into her cunt. It's hot, tight, clenching me, calling me.

She feels like mine.

She's not.

Guilt churns in my belly. I shut my eyes, focusing hard on what's here, instead of what's not.

Hardening my jaw against memories, I twist my hand, and lever my finger forward deep inside her. I feel her body coil up as if it were my own, winding tighter, tighter. I'm doing the same, my dick so thick I've got no choice but to reach down, frantic, and release it from the grip of my pants.

The rough ground hurts, even through my underwear, but that's never stopped me. Pain's just another escape. Something to focus on when shame threatens.

We go on like this for I don't know how long. Probably a couple minutes, with me humping the ground, my fingers fucking her cunt, my mouth open against her pussy. Without warning, she curves in on herself, clamps down on me, and threads her hands into my hair.

My hair.

Automatically, I pull away. She could recognize me and then...

Then what?

Potential complications race through my head, one after another—the moments that led to this full anonymity—women wanting more, pushing too hard, moving for a relationship, when relationships aren't possible anymore. Regret swamps me. I shouldn't have agreed to a second time. No matter how badly I wanted it.

She reaches again and I twist my head to the side, though my hand's still working her hard.

It's different now, though. I'm not lost to the need and the connection I imagined between us and though I'm still hard, I'm ready for it to end. I'll get out of here, head home, work my body out some other way. On the heavy bag, or a new project. There's a chunk of granite in the barn, just begging to be banged into submission.

Detached, I concentrate on her g-spot, playing her like an instrument.

She's no different from the other women, I realize. I mean how could she be? We don't know each other. I've touched her body. She's taken mine. That's all.

"Please," she says, her voice breaking in the middle of the word. And again: "Please, please, please."

Man, do I like the way she sounds.

It takes five, maybe ten quick strokes before she's coming.

I ache to come with her. So badly it hurts.

Ignoring my own need, I finish out her climax, prolonging the last few pulses of her pleasure. I want to savor the gush of her release, shove my whole face against her, let her mark me the way my teeth marked her thigh, but I can't do that and still keep ahold of the dregs of myself.

I wait out her trembling, stroke her leg through the come-down, keeping my body away from her heat. She shuffles to the side to sit up and moves slightly back.

"Can I recipro—"

"No."

"Oh. Right. Okay."

I don't wait for her to stand before pulling the shorts up her legs, feeling around for her shoes and threading them onto her feet.

"Need anything?" *Like a little aftercare, you dick?*

"I'm good." She sounds surer now, hardened. Probably for the best. "Thanks."

I nod. Saying you're welcome after what just happened would be pretty callous. I've become a prick, sure, but I haven't lost my humanity.

At least I don't think so.

I open my mouth to tell her good night, but she beats me to it.

"You can go. I'm...good on my own." What was she about to say there, instead of good? Better off, I'd guess.

And it's true. She will be better off on her own.

Anyone would.

That's why I do things this way. Once or twice a year, at camp, I fuck a woman in the dark. One woman, one time. That's the rule. Anonymous, unemotional physical gratification. No repeats. No goddamn repeats.

I put out my hand and take it back again. She doesn't want it. Of course she doesn't. Christ, what am I doing? Why is this hard?

"Good night," I whisper, choking back the big, oily thing that lives in my chest.

"Bye."

I leave.

And that's it.

That's fucking it.

11

Grace

I GET up and brush myself off, totally alone in the woods.

This was different. It was more. Of *everything*.

Although, weirdly, heartbreak's the only part I can identity right this second.

Almost numb, I pick my way over to the lit path, half smile at the woman working security for this scene a hundred yards up.

I tell her we're done and walk back to the tent, as if that's that.

And it is, isn't it? Done. Over.

I came, he left.

Silly Grace. What more was I hoping for?

Max isn't at the Thunderdome, which is probably for the best, since she'd see right through me if she were. She'd know that it didn't feel right, she'd see that I want to cry, maybe somewhere beneath the fake smile I'd try to put on, and then she'd say something easy and calm and comforting and I'd sob like a baby.

I don't need that. I enter the big tent, thinking I'll just take a second to be alone, maybe, or at least to change out of my now-filthy clothes. It's hot in here, the humidity weighing me down like a wet a blanket. I peel off my shirt and stuff it into the bottom of my bag. Fucking lace doilies at the shoulders. As if he'd ever notice something like that. What is wrong with me?

I rip off my shorts and panties and immediately smell myself on the air. My breath hitches at the memory of his face pressed hard into my core. For a minute, I thought he'd suffocate. Instead, he grunted and gasped and dug deeper.

In the space of a second, desire floods back in, lined with something heavy as lead and bleak like knowing you've lost someone and won't ever get them back.

Stark naked, I flop onto my bed.

I didn't lose anyone tonight.

So, what even was that? What happened out there? The way he caught me, the prolonged fight that seemed to rev him up as much as it did me. I run my hands over my hot, clammy skin. Shoulders bruised, arms scraped, hips sore, knees rubbed raw. Between my legs, I'm wet, swollen, and abused, in the best possible way.

My body shivers at the memory of giving in, going limp for him, and the way he rewarded me for yielding. The sounds he made.

He enjoyed it. There's no doubt about that.

Then why didn't he finish? Why didn't he let me sink to my knees the way I imagined and suck him. I wanted that. I wanted to take him deep, to show him how good he felt. I wanted...

Oh, hell, I don't know. You know what? Maybe, I won't care.

I'm done trying to figure out what makes guys so butt hurt all the damn time.

That's right.

I reach for something clean to put on. They're incomprehensible, especially the ones I can't see or hear or touch. Mr. Stranger Man, whoever he is, just did me a huge favor. If tonight had ended on a high note, I'd have tried to see him again and then maybe he'd have rejected me outright and that's not something I need right now. Been there, done that just two months ago. I'm good, thanks.

It's not like this week's ever been about finding a long term play partner. It's about doing it—okay, so maybe more than once, but whatever—and moving on. That's it. I'm done.

A little more pleased with myself, I throw on a tank top and a clean pair of shorts, foregoing underwear entirely, and head back out into the night, just taking the time to grab my pad and pencil from my bag.

Fuck it, I'm going to the Dungeon.

Liev

Heading home was a bad idea.

Despite the changes I've made this past year, Helen's still everywhere. Her house, her garden. There are nudes of her all over the walls—not by me—art and antiques she bought, collecting dust. I finally got rid of the closet full of clothes, the shoes, perfume, candles. All the accoutrements of my wife's life on earth. Even so, three years out, my feelings are complicated.

I'm used to being a little off when I come inside, but I'm not used to feeling like a cheater who needs to shower before sliding into bed.

Then again, I usually avoid the bed altogether. I prefer the guest room and most nights, I work until I pass out on the sofa in my studio.

I head over to the bar in search of something to dull the ache. No bourbon tonight. I go instead for the single-malt Helen's father gave me that last Christmas we spent together. The last time she could stand on her own.

I break the seal and blow the dust from one of the cut crystal glasses my wife would take out for guests and pour a hefty measure. The burnt peat smell wafts up and washes hot over my eyes.

Fuck it.

I pour a second dose, filling the glass almost to the brim.

Before the burn turns to tears, I head back out to my front porch where I slump into the rocking chair and sip my scotch.

Better. I'm not alone here, with the cicadas and whatever else is singing its ass off tonight. From farther down comes the low thrum of some kind of electronic music. Probably from the Dungeon, where people are happily getting their rocks off, without sadness or guilt or any of the other shit I keep carrying around like a fucking cross.

I've been to therapy. I know I'm not to blame for Helen's death. I know I didn't give her cancer. Nothing more I could've done to save her in the end, but fuck if it doesn't feel wrong to enjoy life when there's nothing left of my wife but ashes.

I take a good swig of scotch, so fine I imagine I can taste the barrel it aged in, then cough against the searing heat.

Actually, the tasting the barrel thing's a lie. It's something I might have said around Helen and her family or any one of her many friends. The fact is, I've got nowhere near the palate I'd need to tell something aged 8 years from 18.

Bet I could pick out my mystery woman's pussy blindfolded.

The thought shoots through me and I'm instantly hard again. I shut my eyes on the twinkling lights spread out below, and breathe in and she's there, on my face, on the fingers I've got wrapped around the glass. Her scent mingles with the whisky into a blend made just for me. I let my head fall back and sip, remembering everything.

After a while, I get restless and go to my studio, where I flip on the overheads and head right to the hunk of granite that's been watching me from the corner these past few weeks, refusing to give me a clue as to what it's meant to be.

I slip on my mask, grab my chisel and hammer and, without hesitation, knock off a corner, then another, turning around the damn thing like a fucking demon. This rock and I are in tune, unlike the goddamn obelisk behind me, where every smack of hammer to chisel was like pulling teeth. This is a meditation that hasn't felt right in ages. Years. The tap of metal to metal, the scrape of chipping stone, then its plink onto the concrete floor. The music's there, just like the shape beneath. It'll be days before it's recognizable, but I know what's here, beneath the layers. I see it already.

I see *them*, with perfect clarity.

Us.

Probably half an hour into the project, the door creaks, breaking the spell. "Whoa. Shit."

I turn to see Zion Mason, known as just Zed in the kink world, standing in the doorway.

"You look like crap, Z."

"Fuck off." Laughing, he stalks inside, dropping his bags like he lives here—which he basically does when he's not shooting movies or the show he's starred in for the last few years. "Come here, you big grumpy asshole." There's no avoiding a hug, so rather than fight it, I wrap my arms around him and clap him hard on the back, accepting the same from him. As always, he tightens his hold and sways a little, keeping the hug going.

When I finally twist away, his face stays close to mine. "What's that?" he says, backing off just when I think I'm gonna have to shove him.

"What?" I wipe at my cheek, figuring it's dust or dirt or some other work shit, then narrow in on the leaf in his hand.

"On your face."

"A leaf?" I put all the disbelief I can into my voice.

He shakes his head. "Pussy."

I go still.

"You smell like fresh pussy, Liev." He holds up the crushed brown leaf, twirling it like a daisy. "You've been rolling around in the woods." He cocks his head when I don't respond. "Who is she?"

"No idea."

"Bullshit."

"Seriously. I don't know."

"You don't go down on your one-offs."

I swallow, feeling trapped on the one hand, but also... "I don't. Not usually." *Free.* "This one's different." How did those words pop out?

"Oh, yeah?" His perfectly-shaped right eyebrow flicks up in one of the signature moves that's made him TV's favorite detective. "Well, she sure smells good. Come here." The bastard grabs my arm and leans in as if to catch another whiff of my face and I scoot back, shoving him at the same time. "Awwwwwww, hoss! Come on. Give me another hit. So, you gettin' it on the regular? She a nice girl? Or is she a dirty little slut who wants you to share her with your best friend? You gonna let me get my face in that—"

"No." My voice lands like a boulder between us.

Zion straightens up, losing the smile. "You're serious."

I want to groan, because he thinks this is an actual thing and when I tell him she wouldn't be able to pick me out from a crowd, he'll laugh his ass off, but here's the thing about Zion—he's not someone I lie to. Ever. And he doesn't lie to me.

So, when I look him right in the eye and say, "I'm never seeing her again. Twice was a mistake," he nods as if he believes me.

"Sure, man." For an interminable handful of seconds, he keeps that slow nod going, his nearly black eyes peeling me apart. "Okay." He looks around. "I went to the house first. Saw you've moved stuff, finally. Cleaned it, too."

At my nod, he grabs my forgotten glass from the windowsill, lifts it in a silent toast, and slugs back the hundred dollar whisky in one swallow. "Good. Now, let's go to the Dungeon."

I don't even bother arguing. There's no point. Zed always wins.

Besides, maybe I don't mind the idea of mingling, for once. Or that a small piece of me is in fact desperate to head back to camp tonight. For reasons.

12

Grace

I shove open the heavy door and let my eyes acclimate to the light here which, though dim, is still brighter than outside. Immediately, my gaze lands on a cage, where a naked, collared person strains to suck a cock that's just outside his reach. I turn away and concentrate instead on a woman in a wheelchair, receiving what looks like the equivalent of a lap dance from another woman. They're sort of chatting as it goes. They kiss, one pinches the other's nipple, then giggles. Beside them, a couple is cuddling on the floor in the corner, lazily eyeing the people around them, without any apparent plan. They're on-lookers like me.

I walk farther in, only letting my eyes settle on a scene for a few polite seconds before moving on to the next. There's music and moaning, the sound of whips and chains, the occasional scream, and laughter. Lots of laughter.

Here's the thing I found out about the Dungeon on my first night here: it's just a huge playroom for adults. Some play house, some tag, others wrestle like puppies. There's peeing in inappropriate places, acrobatics, bullying, humor.

I'm not entirely comfortable here, though that's more about me than the people playing or watching or waiting their turn. I feel like an outsider. I am an outsider, because the kink world's not mine. I mean, yes, I guess I'm kinky.

Inner eyeroll.

Fine. I know I'm kinky. That's been confirmed. Not just by the fantasies, but by the carrying out of them.

By the wanting to do it again and again.

I flinch as my eyes skim over another cage—this one bigger, and filled with people getting pulled around and slapped and otherwise abused—to a padded bench, where a woman is arched back, her ass rosy from being whipped by a man in nothing but a pair of jeans.

Immediately, I focus in on his denim-covered bottom half. Holy shit. Is that my stranger?

Jealousy rips through me at the idea. When the

man unzips and starts to pull his hard dick out, I turn away, so quickly I bash into a big body.

Two big bodies.

My mumbled "Sorry" goes unnoticed by the shorter, wider man, who's already turned his back to me, but the other—a tall, golden-skinned man in a mask that covers everything but his mouth—takes my shoulders in his steadying hands, and smiles. "No worries. You okay?"

My eyes slide from his lush mouth, over a finely-chiseled, clean shaven chest, to the blond happy trail disappearing into a pair of very expensive jeans.

I blink, automatically smiling up at him.

A quick look at the other man's departing back shows that he's in jeans, too. So, maybe denim's not as uncommon as I'd imagined. Although that wide back looks about right. Maybe the hair, too... I'm the prince looking for the glass slipper.

"Yeah," I finally tell the tall man smiling down at me. "Sorry about that."

"You running from something?" One of his hands lingers at my shoulder. I know the second his eyes catch sight of my tattoo, following the thorny stem's progress from my sleeve, down my biceps and forearm to disappear around my wrist. "Wow. That's beautiful work."

I smile automatically. "Thanks."

"What's your name?" Masked guy sounds casual, but there's something a little intense about his interest.

I eye him. Creepy, not particularly. Interested, yes.

Unlike the stranger who licked me to orgasm and left me alone to get dressed.

"Grace," I say, my chin lifting with what feels like childish defiance.

"I'm Zed." He puts out a hand and I shake it, feeling not a single callus on his perfectly soft, dry skin. It's disappointing.

"You here with someone?"

"Max. You know her?"

"Mad Max? Sure. Yeah. She's amazing. She your partner?" He bends forward as if sharing a secret. "Or one of 'em?"

I shake my head, purposely not thinking of my stranger in the woods. "I'm unattached."

"Nice." He smiles wider, his eyes skimming my wrist for a sign of what I'm into. "Newbie, huh?"

"Is it that obvious?"

"Yeah. But you're also wearing a first year bracelet." His head cants. "So, what's your poison?"

"Huh?"

"What would you write on your Camp Haven profile, Grace of the beautiful, sad eyes?"

My pulse picks up. A compliment will do that, I guess. Although, sad? "I'm..." *Say it! Own it!*

Dammit, I want to, but I came here thinking it would be one and done, not the start of a new existence. Am I an actual practicing kinkster now? Is that something I'll need to add to the old resumé?

"Curious? Open?"

"Yeah," I reply, relieved. "Just figuring it out, I guess." I let my eyes wander back to the original denim guy by the bench. He's fucking the woman now and the sight hits me in the solar plexus. It's the way he pulls out, then presses back in, his face absolutely stoic, his body stiff, almost unmoving, while she writhes as much as she can with her legs shackled open. They're less than ten feet away. I almost can't believe I'm a part of this.

It's suddenly overwhelming in here—the sights and sounds, but also the too-intimate smells of sex and sweat and latex and the weight of Zed's attention.

"I'd better, uh..." I turn and scan the room, hoping I'll find Max and she won't be in the middle of getting strung up and beaten and whatever other blissful activities she's got lined up for tonight.

Zed's knowing gaze flicks over me lingering at the glaring scrapes on my knees. "You here all week?"

"I'm not sure."

"Fair enough. You mind if I come by and say hi sometime?"

Excitement flickers in my chest. "Sure. I'm staying with Max. At the Thunderdome."

"That's one of the glamping sites, right?"

At my nod, he opens his mouth as if to say something else, but apparently catches sight of someone behind me and stops.

I turn and see the third denim-clad guy that I

bumped into, wearing his ratty T-shirt, his longish hair tousled and dusty-looking. He's surveying the room from a spot just out of the fray, at the edge of the shadows, his thick arms crossed over a massive, heavily-muscled chest.

Watching him, something stirs deeper inside me —in my brain or my body—it comes and goes so fast, I can't begin to explain it. Do I know him from someplace?

Wait. Is that *him*? The possibility shimmers through my veins until I realize that I *have*, in fact, seen that man before. I glimpsed him this morning at the coffee shop. God, it feels like eons ago.

"He looks pissed, doesn't he?" With a smirk, Zed points the man out with his chin—as if I could miss him. "See him? Arms crossed. Resting bastard face."

I'm not comfortable with staring, but I can't deny the compulsion to give him another quick look, then another. "Not pissed, exactly."

"No? What would you call that expression?"

The man catches us watching him, shakes his head and looks away, as if annoyed or bored, although the next time I glance over, our eyes meet and there's a snap of something in the air.

You, my body thrums. *You you you.*

He looks away, totally uninterested.

Oh. Okay. Maybe not. I feel silly. Disappointed.

"You meet him yet?"

"That guy?"

"The Overlord," Zed intones in a movie trailer voice.

I look up at him. "The *Overlord*?"

"This is his place. All of it."

Him? I dare another quick glance, for which I'm again rewarded—or is it punished?—by a crackle of... interest? Attraction? Is that what this is? I mean, I like the way he looks, I guess. Definitely more my speed than this tall, dimpled, cocky situation that Zed's got going on, with his neatly trimmed body hair, the easy, white smile, and muscles that are way too artfully strung over his taut, towering frame.

He's hot, yes, but *that* man...

I give the Overlord another furtive glance. God, you'd need a bulldozer to move someone like that.

"His place?" I murmur, not understanding and barely aware of the crowd flowing past, the kinksters playing dirty games, the low thrum of music—everything but the presence of that man, bored in his corner, unaffected by it all. A woman stops and winds her arms around his neck, drawing his attention away. He peels her off him, gentle, but firm, and turns away. A minute later, someone else appears beside him, gushing at him effusively, which even I can see from this distance is about as effective as water splashing on rock.

"Yeah. So... You're curious, huh? Curious is good." Zed's leaning down to watch me in a way I don't like at all. It's not lascivious in the least. No, that wouldn't bother me nearly as much as the...

shrewd look he's giving me. *I know what you are*, it seems to say. *I know what you're doing here.* "I'll look for you at some point, Grace," he says with a wink before cutting into the steadily-moving stream of people on his way to meet his friend.

I don't watch him go and I definitely don't let myself look at that other man. I want to, but I don't.

Instead, I find the nearest door to the outside, shove it open, and gulp in huge breaths of humid night air before tromping back to the Thunderdome, where rather than pass out in my fancy tent as planned, I put pen to paper and let all my pent-up emotions flow.

13

Grace

I THINK about putting up another note the next day. I know, I know. I shouldn't.

I should live in the moment and let what happened happen and move on, but I can't. I mean, I will, but I don't want to.

I want to see him again. Well, not see, but feel. Touch, listen. I want to be near him again. I want to be taken up against a tree. On the ground. Wherever we fall.

"Maybe you should play with someone else," Max suggests when I tell her my thoughts. "There are other Primals, Grace. Plenty of guys here would be more than happy to fulfill a forced sex fantasy, even if it's more yours than theirs.

Maybe she's right.

Max, a therapist in her day job, and pretty much a sage in a general way, has been the most supportive person in my life these past few years. She's the one who stuck with me through my parents' accident. At 21 years old, I went from a care-free art student with dreams of inking people in my own tattoo studio, to a full-time caretaker whose only purpose was to keep my mother alive and the two of us afloat.

"This is a vacation, too, Grace, don't forget. Your first in forever. Go crazy. Swim in the pool or something. Or, hey, you should go to the Masquerade soiree tonight."

I perk up. "What's that?"

"Ooooooh, Rose*bud*. Look at you!" Max slides her feet into a pair of well worn hiking boots. She's gone full on Lara Croft gear today, complete with some kind of cross-body holster in which she's slid water and gatorade and what looks like one of those Leatherman multi-tools. "All excited to slip on a mask and get it on in the sex hall?"

Do I want that? "Maybe."

"It's basically just a masked ball. There'll be lots of little secret spaces where people can do fun things. It's all weird and mysterious." She jiggles her eyebrows. "I'll loan you something to wear."

When Max completes her look with round goggle sunglasses straight out of a post-apocalyptic film, I see exactly how she got her name. "Sure you don't want to come hiking?"

"Nope."

Her grimace ruins the look, but it makes me laugh. "We're literally going out into the woods to get it on, Gracie. How is that not what you love?"

"Too many people."

"There'll be people tonight."

"Did you not say something about large object insertion?"

"I did." She snags the water bottle from her holster and licks the cap."

"I'll pass." I do my best not to show my discomfort. No point yucking on my bestie's yum, right?

"Okay. Well, try to get into some trouble while I'm gone."

She presses a loud kiss to my cheek before sauntering away, all confidence and joy.

A couple trans friends of Max's stroll by, holding hands. They wave casually, their smiles friendly. I smile back, barely noticing their nudity, but sort of entranced by how content they look. Immediately, I reach for my sketchbook, doodling happy-looking people with massive smiles.

I draw the lush layers of trees overhead, then let my eyes slide down the skyline to where the forest is darker and mysterious. What is that? I lean forward and squint at what appears to be a boulder. Nah, the shape's too regular for that. After a couple minutes of squinting and sketching, I realize with a jolt that it's a sculpture of a large human head and it's staring right this way. It's too close to a group hard at play, but once they leave, I'll investigate.

I need to see it close up.

I flip the page and, without intending to go there, draw pieces of last night. Dark background scratched deep into the paper, a woman, tall and scared, her shoulders curved under the weight of fear and other inexplicable things. With an indrawn breath, I hint at a shape—more shadow than human.

Something makes me look up again at the sculpture lurking in the shadows across the way. There's a heft to it that draws my eye like a magnet. I scrub my pencil at an angle, working to give my shadow man that same rough texture. It seems right for him, sort of brutal and raw.

The Overlord springs to mind.

I squirm, the drawing forgotten in my lap. A few minutes later, I get up, a little self-conscious, and head into the tent, zipping it shut behind me.

I spend half the day in there masturbating and emerge in need of food and a shower. I grab a quick sandwich from our supply and head over to the shower cabin. Like everything here, it's a shared space, all genders combined.

Luckily for my sense of modesty, it's empty when I arrive. I hang my towel and clean clothes on the wall and juggle my toiletries into one of the few enclosed stalls, then undress inside. The shower's hot, the water pressure hard. It's heavenly to get clean after all I've done. I shut the water off and wrap up in my towel.

Something clangs rhythmically beyond the closed curtain of my stall. It takes me a few heartbeats to figure out that someone's hammering at a pipe and a few more to realize that it's not some kink thing—it's a plumbing thing. Feeling foolish at the slight fear I felt for a second, I reach out for my clothes.

They're not there.

Okay, now I panic. I'm in nothing but an old towel that barely covers my privates, so I can't go out and check, not with someone working what sounds like a few feet away.

I reach out again, patting the wall where I'm sure I left my stuff. Shit. Why isn't it there? The hook's empty. I look around, feeling like I've stepped into another dimension, knock my shampoo onto the floor, then immediately follow that with my razor. The handle lands at my feet, but the head shoots off who knows where. "Shit."

The clanging stops.

I stand still. It's silly, right? They know I'm in here. They're not there to *get* me. I'm just…

Hiding, apparently, in the stall, wearing nothing but a too-small towel.

"Here." I jump at the sound of the low voice.

"Um, yeah?"

"Got your razor. You want to grab it, or…?"

"Oh. Thank you." I pull the curtain back just

enough to pass my hand through, hesitate, and then tense up when something touches me.

What I initially think is a man's hand is, in fact, just the safety blade, being held out. When I cup my hand, he drops it in and I pull back.

I don't move.

He doesn't either. "You okay in there?"

"Yes. Yeah. Thanks. Sorry."

"Nothing to be sorry for."

I open my mouth to disagree, then shut it.

"You looking for your clothes?"

"Yes."

"Right here. Second hook."

Shaking a little, I snap the blade into its base and set it on the ledge. I feel foolish, like the ultimate in uncool.

"Want me to hand 'em in?"

"I'm good. Thanks." I swoosh the curtain open in time to see my savior's wide back as he walks back towards the sink. I recognize the man from the Dungeon last night. Not Zed, the other one. The one I spent way too much time thinking about in my tent today.

The Overlord. He's in jeans again and work boots, looking nothing like the boss. My eyes slide down his wide shape, taking in paint stains and burn marks on fabric and skin. I get stuck staring at a hefty, scarred forearm that's lined with muscle and veins. The hair is dark and looks soft, though everything else about him seems coarse.

He comes to a stop in front of the sink he's clearly working on. My gaze shifts to the half-fogged mirror and runs smack into his.

Oh, crap!

Feeling as though I've been zapped, I swipe the curtain closed, only to be swamped right away by embarrassment. *What now, genius?*

I need my clothes to get dressed, but they're too far to reach without opening the damn curtain again.

I shut my eyes and lean against the side of the stall. Could I not be a little more like Max, for once in my life? Maybe.

When I open my eyes again, I see movement through the sliver left between the curtain and the wall. I watch the man dip to the floor, tighten something, then stand up again to turn on the faucet. He doesn't care about me, right? I'm by far one of the place's lesser attractions. I mean, look at me, hiding in the bathroom like a scared animal or something.

While the faucet's still running, I tighten the towel around my chest, open the curtain all the way, and step out. See? He's not watching me anymore.

I grab my clothes, breath still shaky, turn around and close the curtain, not daring to look his way until the very last second. But when I do, all my breath leaves me in a rush because he *is* watching and his eyes...

Holy shit. My palm slams to my open mouth, keeping in the sounds my frantic lungs are trying to make.

His eyes. Those eyes.

They're seared into my memory, even with the curtain closed, they're as clear as sun spots: blue, bright and intense, their focus so sharp I can't believe they haven't sliced through the bright yellow plastic hanging between us.

It takes a while to catch my breath and get dressed—half because I'm shaking and half because I can't stop listening for him. I hear tools clang while I snap my bra on over painfully sensitive nipples, something scuffs while I drag my shirt on, footsteps while I pull my pants up. Then, in the harsh silence between my quick, overloud heartbeats—nothing.

When I finally emerge, I'm relieved to see that he's gone.

Weird, though, how relief feels almost exactly like disappointment.

14

Liev

I know I've made a mistake the second I agree to go to the masquerade thing with Zion.

"Wait. Say that again."

I roll my eyes. "Don't make me change my mind."

"Okay." He turns and bends to look in the bathroom mirror, sliding mascara onto his long, movie-star lashes. I can tell he's biting his tongue to keep from asking about this uncharacteristic decision. It's a good thing, because I frankly don't have a reply. "You wearing that?"

I look down at the clothes I barely remember putting on this morning. Jeans. T-shirt. "What?"

"Liev. This is *your* camp. Maybe try classing it up a bit."

The idea of getting gussied up is exactly the opposite of what I want right now. Distraction. That's all I need—something to think about other than the shit I've been wondering all day—like, is her hair dark like the woman in the shower? Or, hell, maybe it's grey, maybe she's decades older than me.

Maybe it's time to stop thinking about it.

"At least change that."

I blink at Zion, who's pointing at a white plaster stain cracking on my T-shirt. Annoyed—more at myself for even bothering than at him—I stomp to my bedroom, not once looking at the untouched bed. I open a drawer and pull out the first shirt I find, throw it on, and head downstairs. "I'll be on the porch."

He mutters something and slowly follows, looking admittedly dramatic in tonight's getup. Chest bare aside from a leather harness and nipple rings, he's wearing tight, shiny vinyl pants, tied closed at the waist for easy access. In one hand, he's got a full-coverage black mask, in the other he's holding a slew of leather handcuffs.

"What do you need all those for?" I ask as we set off for the Sex-o-drome tent.

"I was thinking I might start a collection."

"Of cuffs?"

He smiles at my silly question and accompanying eyeroll, hands me the cuffs, and pulls his mask on.

Mine's in my pocket. It's a half-mask, just for show, since I'm not playing tonight.

The music's blasting so loud, we hear it almost right away. By the time we get to the big tent, there's no conversation to be had. Just a steady, electronic heartbeat, picking up and letting out, up and out. We push open the front curtain to see bodies everywhere. Zion immediately dives into the writhing mass.

I turn to go, but the crowd's pushing in, making a quick exit impossible. I hate this. Too many people. It's claustrophobic, despite the air above our heads. The hot mask doesn't help. I use my bulk to forge a path through all the flesh, planning to make my way over to one side, where the tent's open to the night air.

It takes forever—or, hell, maybe just a minute or two stretched out by my misery—to escape the squirming pile of dancers, past a flowing fabric curtain, and into the next area. Here, lush silks hang everywhere, creating a sort of snaky labyrinth of pseudo-intimate spaces. Scattered, low cushioned benches provide more than enough areas to get up to no good.

Which is exactly what's happening. It smells like sex in here. Like sweat and plastic and hot, hungry bodies.

I can't help the way my dick responds, the sudden heaviness in my balls. There's ass-biting and cock-sucking, face-fucking and a whole slew of kinksters getting spanked. Helen would have loved this shit. She'd have been right there in the middle of it, laughing and moaning and opening her arms and legs for whatever new sensation came her way.

A bitterness coats my throat. I swallow it down and shove past another curtain, then another and another. Mirrors on the ceiling reflect the light from chandeliers, others on the wall turn the scene into something from a fun-house. I look right and stutter to a stop, confused when another masked body keeps moving. Shit, that was weird. It's another guy in long pants, wearing a ski mask. He's shirtless, but aside from that, he could be me. Or a taller, narrower version.

And I'm not in the full mask tonight.

Someone touches me. I scoot to the side to let them by, feeling so overwhelmed I can't move. Fuck. I need to get out.

I fling aside another curtain, this one yellow like the ones in the showers. I'm reminded of the woman today—the moment our eyes met in the mirror. How the connection sent an unexpected zing of pleasure through me. Not wanting to scare her, I tamped it down and got out of there fast.

Across the room, someone moves quickly, almost running. It's someone with long, dark hair flowing around their shoulders. Is it her? My mystery woman? A black tattoo curves out from her sleeve to wind around her arm. I saw that tattoo beaded with water today.

She's gone in a flash, but that was her. Maybe.

Probably. I fight the desire to chase her and concentrate instead on getting out. I turn and catch sight of another woman. Red mask. Lace cat suit. She could fit the bill. I scan her arm. No inked trail of thorns. Not my shower woman. But what about my mystery play partner?

I look back to where the first figure disappeared and consider getting closer, just to see, then catch sight of myself in the mirror.

Jesus, what am I doing? This isn't a scene. That's *not* a play partner. She's a random woman who freaked out when she saw me fixing a damn sink.

That's it. I'm getting out of here before I do something I'll regret.

Grace

I see him almost the minute we get to the Masquerade Soirée: a man in a dark, soft T-shirt and jeans, wearing the kind of ski mask he had on last night.

I don't think he notices me at first, but it's him. I know it. There's something about the smooth, predatory way he walks around the space, always watching, always moving.

There's something a little unnatural about me doing the stalking, but after a while I suspect that my undivided attention sounded some deep, instinctive, animal alarm, because he turns and stares right at me.

A full body shiver shakes me, from my borrowed carnival mask, over the T-shirt I've tucked into Max's long, red tutu, to the toes of my sandal-clad feet.

His eyes narrow behind the mask, his body tenses. I feel a responding tautness in my own, count to three under my breath, and take off.

Between dancing bodies, under swaying cages, complete with human songbirds in nothing but paint, around benches that are too obscene for me to look at, through curtain after curtain after curtain, I race, my heart and body thrumming from the thrill of it.

I smack into someone. He steadies me. "Hey, there, Grace."

It's the tall guy from last night, I think. "Hi," I have to yell to be heard over the booming music.

I look over my shoulder.

"It's Zed." He leans close, stares behind me, then back to me. "You okay?"

"Yeah. Yeah." Another quick scan of the crowd. Oh. There! There he is, coming toward me, moving fast. "Gotta go."

I take off, smack into a group of people watching something. I can't look. I won't look. Oh, shit. Needles. I spin away, knock into someone else, peek back and see Zed block my pursuer's path in a way that looks fumbling and inept, but...

I narrow my eyes. Is he doing it on purpose?

My stalker throws an elbow at Zed and continues, his progress frightening and inevitable.

He's gaining on me, which my body feels so keenly, I want to moan.

I swerve, push another curtain out of my way, and run into a bench.

Dead end.

I take two steps back the way I came and run smack into him.

"Hey." His hands go to my shoulders. "Wanna play?" he yells above the music. His voice is not what I expected.

The hands on my shoulders are hot, a little clammy.

"Yeah."

"Yes?"

"Yes!" I yell through the too-loud beat. I nod and give a smile that feels wooden and fake—the way I'd smile at a cop who's busy scrawling out my speeding ticket.

"What do I call you?"

Oh. I hadn't thought of that. Should I give my name? "Rosebud," I spit out in a rush of inspiration.

I think he smiles. I can't tell with the mask. "Cute. I'm Blade."

"Hi."

"You like being hunted, huh?"

"Yes. Yeah." I'm breathing hard, a little excited, a little nervous.

"I'm a Primal. You want to mess around? Just hang out here. Wrestle or something. On the bench?"

This isn't my stranger. I know it. Then again, the stranger's not actually mine, is he? That's not a thing and maybe this is. Or it could be. I'm going to try. Maybe a new partner is what I need. "Yes."

"You got hard limits you want me to stay away from?"

My mind goes blank. I glance at the people around us. Limits? "Uh, no anal." But wait. Do I want to have sex right here with this person? Do I want to do this in front of everyone else?

I turn to look at the cushion-covered bench.

"You got your...?"

The music blares louder, making me lean in. "What? I'm sorry, I can't hear."

"Safe word?"

"Oh. Yeah. Yeah, it's Red."

"Okay." The eyes behind the mask crinkle. They're nice eyes. He seems fine. The whole thing seems totally, perfectly fine, and yet... "I can't. I can't help feeling that I've got somewhere else to be."

He gives me space. "You okay?"

I'm nodding non-stop. "Yep. Fine, I just... changed my mind."

He puts his hands up. "Yep Okay. Need anything?"

"No. No, thank you." I smile, relieved by the choice I've made. "Goodnight, Blade."

"See you around, Rosebud."

Out in the night, I breathe air and humidity, the smell of trees and dirt.

"Hey."

I huff out a breath at the sound of Zed's voice. "Hi."

"How's it going?"

"I almost got involved in a scene and changed my mind."

"Happens. You need company?"

"No." I inhale more air, let the anxiety trickle away. "I need a walk." My hand goes out to stop him from joining me. "I'm serious fine. Just...weirded out."

"Wanna tell me why?"

I'm shaking my head. "It's silly."

"No such thing."

"I thought he was someone else."

Zed's eyes—the only thing I can see of his face—flick back to the tent. "Not the droid you were looking for?"

A laugh bursts from my lips, sounding just like a bark in the night. "Guess not." I look down at where my sandal's scuffing the grass, and then over towards the woods where I played the last two nights. "Kinda worried I've been ruined for all other droids."

"Ooooooh." I picture a pained expression under the mask. "Tough."

"Anyway." I straighten my back. "I'm gonna..." I point vaguely in the direction of the tents, though I have no intention of going there. "Thanks, Zed."

"Anytime, Grace."

I walk away, slowly at first. The second Zed disappears inside, I change course and veer toward the woods. I can't explain it, but that's where I want to be.

15

Liev

There's no new note at the coffee shop.

I don't care. I'm not looking for more anyway. I need alone time. Time to think, time to just be, instead of *doing*.

I wind up at the camp store—currently closed for the day—and use my key to get in. I slip a six-pack of beer into a canvas Camp Haven tote and add it to my tab.

Back outside, the trill of crickets and cicadas layers over the thrum of music to lull me.

I root around in the bag and pull out a beer, crack it open and take a long, cool sip. I don't want to go home, I admit, already heading in the general direction of my woods.

If I can't be honest with myself at my age, what's the damn point anyway?

And, in the spirit of painful truths, I really shouldn't have gone back with my mystery woman a second time. The second time did it.

Although I suspect the damage was already done.

What good are all the goddamn parameters if I don't stay within them myself?

I swallow more beer, and let myself feel desperate for the woman whose pussy I tasted, whose smell and skin and sounds of pleasure I've got imprinted on my insides.

I can't ask, obviously. First of all, I'm the one who insisted on anonymity. But also rules are rules and if you mess with the basics at a place like Camp Haven, you might as well tear the whole place down.

There's no security volunteer hanging out around the perimeter, meaning no one's doing a scene here tonight.

Thank fuck. She's not out here wrestling around in the dirt with someone else. I blow out air I didn't realize I was holding.

It's a relief, but still my stomach twists. She's probably in the big tent, coming hard on another man's cock. Or tongue. Maybe two men.

Dammit. I attempt to calm myself with beer. A doomed endeavor.

But, fuck, isn't everything? We start dying the

day we're born. Some of us faster than others. Helen had no idea she'd be gone before the age of thirty-five. None of us could have guessed. We should have known. Because from the moment we come into this world, we're doomed. We're all fucking doomed.

I walk deeper into the forest, around big, familiar trunks, between bushes, avoiding roots and vines, until I get to where I caught her last night. Right here, by a maple that's seen more days than my mystery woman and me and Helen put together. It feels right to drop to the ground and sink back against this particular trunk, nestling my loot in the hollow beside me.

It's unclear how much time has passed when I hear something—or someone—moving in the vicinity. Two beers' worth of minutes. In my current mood, it's probably only been half an hour, though it feels like more. Like I've been here for years, or asleep. I've grown roots of my own in this spot.

I cock my head at what is clearly the sound of footsteps, slow and uneven over the ground. Immediately, my heartbeat picks up speed, my senses flash into the hyper-aware, red alert zone that's got my pulse pounding hard in my cock.

Another few steps closer, the crack of something dead and dry on the ground.

For the first time, I get an inkling of how it feels to be prey instead of predator. My dick goes inexplicably harder, as if the idea appeals, when years of doing this prove otherwise.

I didn't come here for company, my mind insists, while my body's already preparing for a fight. The good kind. The kind that ends in a tight cunt clenching around my dick.

A little irritated, I reach down and palm myself, pressing hard in an attempt to stamp out the inappropriate reaction. That's when she speaks.

"This is stupid." I suspect the words aren't meant for me, or anyone else for that matter, but they wrap around me nonetheless, like vines around a tree.

I hold my breath.

She moves, though I can't tell if she's approaching or moving away.

"Ouch. Shit." And then a hard exhale. It's an annoyed sound, followed by what might be an internal argument, happening aloud. "Fine. Fine." A pause. "Hello?" she voices, louder. That shakiness is there, from the first night. It pulls hard at something inside me.

While I cast around for an appropriate response, instead of, *Hey, girl. That you?* or, I don't know, *Boo!*, my hand nudges the cold edge of a beer can and inspiration strikes. With stiff fingers, I pop the pull top, my movements slow, the sound loud as hell and totally out of place here in the wild.

At first, she doesn't respond, which makes me doubt everything, from coming here to begin with, to giving in to the urge to share my presence.

But then, after a prolonged beat, she lets out a

breathy little sound that could be a sigh or a laugh or, hell, even annoyance.

"You're here," she says, to which I can do nothing but drop my head back and wait, drawing deeply from what I think is my third beer.

Her progress toward me is slow. I assume she's giving me time to tell her to beat it or, worst case scenario, escape on my own if I want.

I don't want. At all. I want to stay here. I want to see what happens next.

Grace

With the sliver of moon above, it's lighter out tonight, which lends more depth to the woods, but also, in a weird way, more mystery. I follow his low, grainy whisper, half-convinced it's a dream, to a tree that is all too familiar, though it smells like beer tonight instead of sex.

"Watch your step."

My eyes just make him out on the ground, wedged up against the tree.

"Have a seat."

Using the trunk as a guide, I settle beside him, without quite touching, and lean my head against the rough bark, watching the stars flicker with the movement of the leaves.

I inhale the skunk scent of beer, mixed with moss and pine.

"Drink?"

It's a relief, after the masquerade's mind-numbing racket, to reply in a whisper of my own. "Yeah. Please."

A can opens and a second later touches my arm. I jump, squeak involuntarily, and laugh as I accept the beer. It's a real laugh, which I know isn't part of the anonymity pact, but to hell with it. I won't be staying at camp forever. He won't have to worry about me next week.

"Thanks." Settling back, I look up again.

Our shoulders touch.

I stop breathing, expecting...hell, I don't know. For him to move away? For him to jump me? Any number of things, but certainly not the long, low hum he lets out. It sounds like pleasure, like comfort, and when he presses his arm to mine, it vibrates through him like a purr.

The beer goes down easily—too fast, probably, but I'm nervous, despite our easy silence.

I expect questions, I guess, maybe even accusations. *Why the hell are you back here?* He says nothing, just drinks, leans in so our skulls almost touch. Our arms peacefully co-exist.

After a while, he turns and I go still, my can suspended on the edge of my lip. I'm wet between the thighs, which is a strange, unexpected development, given that nothing sexual has happened.

"I've had too many of these."

"Okay." It doesn't stop my nerves from humming way up close to the surface.

"Do you know who I am?" His question shocks me, each word a puff of hot, hot air against my neck.

"No." At the almost disappointed sound he makes, I half turn, putting my cheek so close to his, I feel the prick of his stubble.

"You have an idea?"

Nodding scrubs my skin to his. "I know who I *want* you to be."

"Yeah, well. Whoever you think I am, it's not me," he says with a depressing finality.

I close my eyes and inhale deeply through my nose. Beer, warm skin, maybe soap in there somewhere. "Give me your hand," I tell him and without hesitation, he moves his can from his one hand to the other.

His skin is cold, the fingers and palm slightly damp from condensation. The rough bits aren't just calluses, they're ridges under my fingers, a bas-relief; a map. I trace each bump, remembering how it felt against my body, then lift his hand to my face. Oh, there it is. I remember this from last night. From the time before, too. Memories flood in with this smell, the way they often do—scrubbing my hands in the big, dirty sink in art class back in school. Watching the paint slough off in little chips and swirl down the drain.

"Lava soap," I tell him, pressing my smile to one thick knuckle.

He stiffens, but doesn't take his hand away.

Slowly, as if the dark will somehow last forever, giving us all the time in the world, I chart every dip of his hand with my lips, test every peak with my teeth, smooth every cut with my tongue.

The man lets me, which is some kind of new moon witchcraft. I'll take it, whatever his reason for staying still.

Laughing at myself, I weigh his hand in both of mine, then feed the tip of his finger into my mouth, lick it, and suck it deep, wondering why I've never found this act sexy before. I get lost like this for a bit, just sucking, licking, tasting.

With a gruff sound, he eases a second finger in.

I accept his offering, shut my eyes and revel in his fascinating topography. This growing hunger will take whatever he wants to give me. He lets me suck him, not moving or shoving or forcing or any of those things I've seen people do to each other this week. Things he's done to me. Things I'd gladly take again.

After a while, something in him wakes up. I feel the change as he takes the exploration both ways. His blunt fingers twist slightly in my mouth, seeking details of their own. They run over my teeth, the insides of my cheeks, and my tongue, finally sliding back far enough to almost gag me. I enjoy the rush of warmth to my sex, a reaction I do not understand in the slightest.

My body's humming with the desire for more—bigger, harder, deeper.

He moves beside me and now his other hand wraps around my throat and I want this. All of it: the tender touches, the familiar smells, my limits being pushed.

His fingers curl up and separate, gagging me. I could stop him right now, but I'm clenching his wrist and keeping him here, right back in that animal place we share.

"This what you want?" he mutters, low and a little angry against my ear.

I nod, helpless to refuse. All I want is the taste of his skin

"You want to be forced to take whatever I give you, here in the dark?"

I choke trying to answer. He pulls his fingers out, spreads their wet caress on my cheek.

"Say it."

"Yes."

"I want to hear what you want. Say it out loud."

Breathing hard, caught between scratchy bark and coarse skin, I look at his wide shape in the dark, open my mouth, and give him the truth. "I want you."

"Goddammit." He sighs. "Come here."

16

Liev

IN THE NEXT BREATH, she's over me, on me, straddling my lap, her hands wrapping around my neck, my fingers already entwined in the long ropes of her hair, holding her to me, keeping her close. Her lips are lush and warm against mine, the kiss so ravenous and raw that for a handful of seconds, spots dance in the air around us.

I crush her soft mouth from below, filled with something more than want, bordering on need and obsession. This isn't a kiss, it's mouth-to-mouth, a revival, an angel dragging me back from the dead. I lick and bite and suckle her tongue. It tastes like cold beer and new beginnings. Like the dead of night dancing with the first strains of dawn. She tastes like a warm, sweet woman whose cunt I've fucked and feasted on, but whose name I don't even know.

I pull away, enjoying the soft suction of lips loathe to let go.

"Haven't done that for a while."

"Kiss?"

"Three years." The admission tumbles from my mouth.

Her gasp twists in my chest.

For a while, we exchange air, listening more than anything else. I fight the urge to lift my hips. I fight the urge to move, to run. I think she's watching me, but we're too close to tell. And the dark wouldn't tell me anyway.

"I've *never* been kissed like this." She moves in, probably in an attempt to see if we can do as well the second time. At the last moment, I angle my head and kiss her cheek, her jaw, then lower—her neck. Sounds flow from her mouth like syrup—a sweet, slow treble counterpoint to the night's frantic bass.

I give in and flex my ass, showing her how hard she's made me, how much I want her—also possibly avoiding more soul-bruising intimacy.

I'm a coward, hiding in the dark.

Mouth suddenly hard, I grip her skirt. It's a long, fluffy cloud of fabric, trapped between our bodies and it's all I can do not to tear it.

"Hold on." Her hand lands light on my shoulder and she shifts, gathers the whole pouffy thing and drags it up to let it pool around us. Then, as if she's read my mind, she moves again, this time allowing access to my fly. When I go to unbutton it, she brushes my hands away. Almost bossy. Like she's in charge.

My growl rolls out from someplace deep and usually quiet. She ignores it in favor of freeing the other beast from my underwear.

Her hands are too careful on my pounding cock. I want her mean, I want scratches and bruises. I want rough, punishing strokes. Instead, she pulls me out like I'm fragile.

I'm about to show her how tight I need it when she bends forward and presses her lips to the weeping tip. This kiss breaks me right down the middle. It tears me in half and there's not a thing I can do about it.

I can't move, my lungs can't take in air, my voice is frozen in my throat. All I can do is strain to see the woman who's stripping me barer by the second.

It's a relief when her tongue joins in. I need her teeth. "Bite it." I just remember to keep my voice to a whisper. She scrapes my skin. I slide a fist into her hair. "Harder."

Instead of doing what I want, she sinks deep, taking half my cock into her hot mouth in one go. I pull her back by the hair and she wrenches herself from my grasp, diving back in for more. She laps at the precum beading at my slit and I grunt, use her hair to hold her. She fights it—oh, yeah—turns and bites me. This time, the teeth scrape just right. The pain's a light in the dark.

I follow it, deeper into this thing that's not anonymous, that's not one-time. That's not ending with a clean, easy break. I follow it because, right now, right here, this light is the only thing I have.

I tug at her hair. She takes me deeper, gagging herself on me.

"What's your safe word?" I hiss, tightening my fist and pulling her off me.

"Red."

"How do you stop me if you're too full of dick to say it?"

She taps me twice on the thigh. "Good."

Say my name.

I clench my jaw, shut my eyes. "Suck it."

In response, she moans and drops right back to what she was doing. Her lower body's swaying, hips working hard to press her cunt to my knee. I can't imagine she's getting much pressure, though the wet spot's soaked through to my skin.

This time, she doesn't kiss or fondle. Her hands don't hold me like before. Instead she works her mouth down and down until she's choking at the widest part. I stroke both hands against her skull, dig my fingers into silky hair that I see in my mind as dark brown ropes, and make her take another inch.

She gags, her throat flutters. Saliva drips hot then cold, coating me, slicking the whole filthy thing. Her head tries to lift and I let it, give her a chance to breathe. She hardly takes it before she's back on me, around me, so hot and tight and wet that it's an effort not to blow.

Another press down, her body writhes for air, the need in my dick is agony.

In this moment, I want more. I find her tit under cotton, twist the nipple through the material and—fuck me—she's pushing harder, bottoming out, clasping me with her throat, giving her body up to my pleasure and it's too much. It's too fucking much.

My head falls back against the tree. I stare dully at the night sky. The stars are so fucking bright, twinkling with some message from space. The leaves scrape and scratch and rustle in the wind, branches dancing with glee.

All around us, there's life. Fuck, it's buzzing, scratching at the surface of me.

I want to come, but not like this. Not alone.

Grace

I'm drunk. Not on beer, but on him. This. Us. It's sex, only not the way I've done it all my adult life—in a bed, quiet and safe and restrained. It's sex the way it was meant to be. At least for me.

For us, I think. Us. Us. Us.

One minute, I'm sucking him deep in my mouth, my throat, every inch of me sunk deep in the morass of this act, which is giving and taking and sharing in a way I've never wanted to do before. I want to give up everything, even oxygen, to this man. No, not to him. To us.

Us. Us. Us.

His big hands pull me off, so gentle, too gentle. I try to get him back—I want that taste on my tongue—but he keeps me at an unbearable distance.

What I feel in this moment isn't strained thighs and raw, stretched lips. It's an ache that needs filling. My mouth, my cunt, my ass. I'd take him anywhere, give him all of it.

"Come here," he whispers and I love the low rasp of his words. It's just for me. Mine.

His grip's firm on my ass, tight and bossy. He moves me up, lining us up so his erection slides me open like a flower. I'm drenched and swollen and aching to be taken, so when his fat head slots itself right where I want it, I push. God, I push. I shouldn't, but I do.

He groans aloud, clamps his hands tighter on my hips, and stops me.

"I don't have a condom."

The devil in me wants to say to hell with it. How easy would it be? I'm on the pill, after all. And he's careful. I know it. I'm sure. So sure, I want take more of him. I stop.

"I... We can't."

My weight settles forward, putting my forehead to his. "I know."

He adjusts, just enough so I feel the penetration. This is bad. I swallow and there's guilt mixed in with the pleasure. It's the bad kind, not the good.

Right. Shit. The fog clears from my sex-addled brain.

I don't know this man. We're strangers. This isn't a mistake I can make.

I screw my eyes shut and pull up and off. "I'm sorry."

"'s okay." His hand strokes my hair, the calluses catching as he goes. "I'm pretty..." He sighs, his chest moving me, shifting our mouths closer together. "You're the only person I've had sex with in eleven months, so..." Another big inhale rocks me back and forward, slicks my wet heat over his.

"Wow." Whatever jealousy I felt at having to share this man with other anonymous women fritters away into nothing but dust. "I'm on the pill. If that makes a difference."

"It does. I mean... It definitely does."

It's my turn to sigh as more brain cells come online. "I got tested before I came here. It all came back negative. And I've never actually done it without a condom before."

"No?" He has, I take it. And just like that, the

jealousy's back. As if there's room for silly little emotions in this uncommon arrangement. God, what a mess I am.

"I want to make this good for you," I tell him.

"It's good."

"It's not what you want. The hunt."

"Isn't it?" With his next words, he breaks my heart. "We shouldn't do this again."

"I know."

He nods, I think. As if to etch our agreement into the bark behind his head. Like our initials with a big line through them.

I have to ask. "Why not, exactly?" *Are you married?*

"It's complicated."

Isn't it always?"

He tilts his pelvis up and grasps me around the waist with one hand, digging his other into my hip and sliding me up and back. Up and back. Under my ass, his jeans are rough, the abrasion not the same as moss or dirt, but just as uncomfortable.

It makes me want more of him—the feel of skin, maybe body hair. The thighs beneath me are thick with muscle that I want to test, press, weigh against my body.

A slick slide of our sexes gives my clit perfect friction. "That's good," I say, wishing I had a name for this man, other than stranger.

And Overlord, if it's even him, really doesn't cut it for me.

"Fuck," he grates out in that raw, animal way that sends shivers up my spine and out to tingle in my limbs. "Move." He grips me tighter, forces my body's rhythm to match his. It's bossy and a little demeaning and it pumps me up that much closer to orgasm. "Come on."

I'm on him, working hard, my legs shaking with the effort and he's pushy in a way I'd resent in real life. Here, it ramps me up, heats my face with something bordering on humiliation.

When he smacks my ass, it coalesces into that stark, driving need. Without conscious thought, I dig my fingernails into his shoulders. What would he do if I smacked him back?

"Harder," he mutters, sounding as lost in this thing as I am. "Yeah." Another slap shakes my ass. Another. His hard cock's sliding now in quick, jerky movements that nudge my entrance and rub my clit. It's the perfect, high wire cocktail. Danger, pleasure, the pain of being spanked, the tight grip of fingers indenting muscle, the bright, unexpected thrill of it all.

Fuck. "I'm coming," I gasp, my body a tool. Nothing but a tool. For his pleasure. For mine. "I'm coming."

"Yeah. Do it. Show me." He's grunting through harsh breaths that I want to consume.

I can't show him, not really. Not the way I want.

Another thrust, another. He reaches one hand

down and pinches my clit—the way only he's ever done. I explode. Hard. Ugly.

I'm so loud he puts his palm to my mouth to quiet me, but I don't care.

I don't care, because I'm flying. This whole thing —from beginning to end—is a dive off a cliff, head first. And I don't care.

I open up my arms and take it. I take it all.

17

Liev

She's just started coming when I press up on my legs, shift my weight and lever us forward. I cover her body and sink my teeth into her neck, giving my aching cock whatever friction I can.

I want to come too, but the need to mark her's stronger. I'm down to the most basic parts: blunt teeth taking soft skin, pressing hard enough to hurt, but not to break it. She's frozen in place while my cock nudges her swollen little clit.

Oh, fuck, she tastes good.

I'm not supposed to love this.

I'm pumping against her harder, faster. Closing

my eyes, I picture her cunt wrapped around me, clamping hard as she comes on my dick and...

Oh, fuck, I'm there. I'm there, my teeth digging in, belly tight, pressure building, spunk rushing up my shaft.

I need more. Fuck. More.

Lost.

"Dammit," I say, my voice raw. I lean back, shove her skirt out of the way, grab her shirt, her bra, drag them up, jerk my cock, and shoot—across her belly, her tits. Probably as far as her face.

I want to see it. I crave it. Hot, white ribbons of come marking her as mine. Savage grunts tear from my lungs, wrack my body, my stiff arm, my tightly clasped fist. One final stroke wrings the last drop of my load and I'm done. Wiped.

It takes ages for me to come down. When I do, my legs are screaming, my ass aching from where the roots dug into muscle. Shit, my back's already so stiff I don't know how the hell I'll stand.

First, though, I roll onto my side, dragging her over me. She's a rag doll, her weight just right on my chest, in my arms. I set my chin on her head and breathe in the sweat and musk of sex, the lingering scent of shampoo that tickles my senses. My memory.

This woman feels like mine.

I want to care for her. Want to hold her, take her home, feed her, give her a bath. Fuck, I want to ease all the pain she's ever felt. Before, now, after.

I shake my head, trying to see something. Her, if I can, though that's wrong.

It isn't how this goes.

Slowly, she shifts, lifts up and looks down, although I can't imagine she can see a thing. "Hi."

I let my hand rub her back, knowing it'll just be harder to let go. "Hey."

"That was..." I picture a face above mine, blinking. The face I see is that woman from the shower. It's fucked up. I know. It's dangerous to assign anything real to this.

With a low laugh, she collapses, which is good. Good that I can stop overlapping a different reality to this stark one.

After a second, she stops shaking.

"You okay?" I pat her back. That should get things moving.

She nods, then breathes in so deeply her belly presses to mine. "Yeah. You?"

I don't know why it surprises me that she's asked. Everything she's done so far is...what I'd do, I guess. Fuck, what is that? She's like holding up a mirror to my face, only better. Like one of those goddamn social media filters Lamé loves so much.

"I'm..." I think about minimizing it, then roll straight into the truth. "Destroyed." *Ruined for anyone else. For always.*

"Yeah. I should go, right?"

No. No, God. I sniff.

"You were...that was..."

"What?" I can't help asking. I'm a weak human, after all.

"Is transcendent a word? That seems like a word."

"It is," I say, my throat tight and weird and fucked from the inside. "It is."

Grace

I kiss him one last time. It hurts. The way too much sugar hurts your teeth and leaves bumps on your tongue.

I get up. My feet are numb, my knees a wobbly mess. I can't stand the idea of saying goodbye. I can't stand it being over.

He sits up, but I make him stay there, his body rooted to the ground when I leave, strong enough to hold me, break me, put me back together.

He's done it all in one night and, as I stumble back towards the light, I'm not sure I'll survive.

I will, I guess. I've gone through worse.

But this is gonna hurt. it's clear as I trip from our darkness back into the too bright world. My shirt sticking to my belly and chest, my skirt floating semi-crushed around me.

I'll apologize to Max. I'll buy her a new one.

Yeah right. She won't want it. She'll be so happy I ruined it she'll frame it on her wall.

A giggle tumbles from me, though it's almost a sob. Then another. This one truly half-and-half. Actually, fuck that. This isn't sad. This is good. It's a fucking lot to deal with, but it's good.

I'm good.

I let my next breath build me up again, give me courage, give me strength. The next is even better. It gives me a spine and a smile.

Someone stumbles by, wearing nothing but a collar and a constellation of bruises. Their glassy gaze meets mine. We share a grin.

I offer an exhausted, "Good night."

"Sweet dreams," they reply.

"Yeah. You, too."

I sail back to the tent on my very own cloud.

18

Grace

I WAKE up feeling tender and wide open, full of bittersweet nostalgia for something that's still flowing in my veins. Still hurts. Still feels good.

The urge to draw forces me to grab my pad, half asleep under my blankets, and sketch out something from my dreams. It's a wolf, outlined in edges rough, but solid. The fact that it's meant to be inked into skin doesn't occur to me until I set it down and stretch my sore body.

Oh my God, I feel abused. Every part of me's aching and strained. My knees look the way they did in elementary school—skinned and scabbed over and skinned again. And, like wounds made while playing as a kid, they're painful, but in the end worth it.

Grinning like a fool, I tiptoe out into the heat of the day, set the electric kettle to boil and promptly forget it when I start sketching again. First, it's a picture of my knees, filthy and scratched and beautiful as a badge of honor. I understand Max's pride, suddenly, in her bruises and pinpricks and rope burns.

Next, I do a jaunty doodle of a tall, very thin white man with a parrot on his shoulder, who dances by to whatever's playing in his earbuds, looking like he's escaped the set of yet another *Pirates of the Caribbean* movie. Then, the little brown birds pecking at the campfire leftovers at the site across the way. I turn the page and make the birds bigger, flip it again and make them people—clothed in scraps, clawing at crumbs on the ground.

I shriek when a shadow leans over my shoulder.

The birds flutter off in a wild flap of wings.

"Sorry," Max says, smelling of toothpaste and sleep. "What's this?" She points at the drawing and it's all I can do not to hide it. It feels too personal right now. Almost sore, like my trophies from last night.

She's watching me with knowing eyes. I sigh and flip it so she can see the picture.

"Wow. Let me see."

I hand her the book, unable to watch her go through the pages.

"Holy shit." She turns it around to show me a

nude, strung up on a cross, face to one side, body half limp from pleasure and pain and exhaustion. "Mistress Mandy's gonna love this. You could sell it to her. Or her sub, but Mandy's gonna go apeshit. Grace, this is incredible. How have you gotten better without practice?" She glances up at me and immediately rolls her eyes. "Please. Just let me give you the occasional compliment, okay? I know you hate it, but—"

"It's fine," I cut in. "Thank you. And, I guess I'm...inspired."

She perks up. "That's great. How long's it been since you picked up a pencil and drew? Or a tattoo gun?"

I give her a wry look. "You know how long."

"Yeah." She hands me back the pad back so I can continue and I immediately sketch in a deep line between the woman's eyes, moving her closer to agony or ecstasy or that liminal place between. "You could make money doing tattoos, you know. You don't have to paint houses."

She's right. I'd need to invest, but that's not been the only thing keeping me away. "It felt weird, after Dad died. You know?"

"Yeah. He was always the one after you to keep up the art stuff."

"Exactly. I didn't much feel like it anymore."

"And now you do," she says, gently. "Keep going, since you're on a roll. I'll go get us fancy coffees and then I'm off to teach my workshop."

"Oh my God! Your dance workshop's today? Wait. Isn't that like, soon?" I hop up. "You go shower. I'll get us coffees."

"Really? You don't mind?"

"Hell, no. I've got to check in on Mom anyway. Go! I've got this." And maybe I'll just happen to glance at the message board while I'm there.

On the way, I pass two people holding hands as they stroll slowly down the path, wearing nothing but boy short underwear and lots of piercings all over. With lazy smiles, they hold up their coffee cups in salute. I wave hello and keep my eyes up, although what I really want is to open up my sketch pad and draw. Now that the seal's been broken, I've gone from zero creativity to non-stop creation.

In a funny way, it doesn't even feel creative. My mind's not making this stuff up, my hand's just drawing what I see. I'm like a conduit or something. It's liberating to not worry about form or content or design and just draw.

I used to love doing this, before art school and the accident. It's like exercising long-neglected muscles. It feels amazing.

There's another stone sculpture by the path near the main building. This one's a writhing knot of naked men, engaging in love or war. Fighting or fucking, so intermingled in this place.

My footsteps slow and—with no one around to see—I stroke a hand down a muscled stone back. Its rough finish feels sensuous beneath my fingertips. I lean in. Up close, I see just how meticulous the work is—the level of detail sort of astounding for a piece this massive, this…brutal. It's so alive, so full of emotion and tension, some of it hums through my own veins.

A little breathless, I walk into the coffee shop to find Lamé doing an acrobatic dance behind the bar, which evolves, when she sees me, into jumping and slithering,

"Hey, girl!"

"Hi." I wave. "Let me send this real quick."

I text my mom for news and wait for the reply. She's fine. I'm fine. Vacation's great.

I don't say dreamy. Dreamy would be a step too far. She'd want details about dreamy.

Details there's no way I can share. Not with Mom, at least.

I look up, finally, to see Lamé watching me with wide-open eyes, leaning forward, elbow on the bar, chin in her hand. "How are you?"

I could make up some crap, but I don't. That's the thing about Kink Camp. The truth comes out eventually.

"I'm kind of…I don't know. Raw?"

Her brows fly up. "Tell me all."

"I saw him again last night."

Her eyes get impossibly wider. "Reaaaaaally?"

"We…made out. God, we did a lot. We talked."

"Talked?" Lamé swoops down the counter, then

back, her skates loud, even with the music. "You talked? Like words?"

"Actual conversation." I watch her frenetic back and forth. "We kissed and then—"

"You *kissed?*" With a yelp, Lamé disappears behind the bar.

I race around to find her on the ground, legs sprawled in front of her, like some hyper-sexualized Bambi, and squat beside her. "You okay?"

"Oh my God!" She's laughing. "I'm such a klutz!"

"You're wearing roller skates."

"Dammit," she moans. "I hate it when he's right."

"Who's he?"

"The boss. He told me I'd put an eye out one day."

"Put an eye out? Those were his words?"

"His exact words."

"He sounds like an eighty-year-old man." I attempt to get her up to standing.

"So, when you say kissed—" About halfway up, she screeches. Immediately, I help her down again. "My ankle. Oh, shit." After recovering, she leans forward to undo the laces, but I'm already there.

"Ice?" I ask, as soon as I've eased the boots off. This is a dance I've done more times than I can count. Sometimes Mom's barely down before I've got her on a flat surface, ice pack out. "Bags? Or a towel?"

"Behind the counter. Bags are on that shelf." Lamé points with one of her sharp, rainbow-painted talons.

"Come on. Let's get you up on a chair. If you think you can."

Once she's all settled, I head over to where I spotted one of those big, professional-looking emergency first-aid kits, drag it over and take out a painkiller and the compression bandage. Lamé watches me. "You've done this before."

I grimace at her ankle, which is quickly swelling. "A time or two."

"Me, too. In another lifetime." She nods and starts to get up. "All right. Now help me to the counter."

"Whoa whoa whoa. Sit down."

"You know how to make coffee? 'Cause I'm not sitting unless you do."

A couple people walk in and wander over, followed by more.

"Anyone know how to use one of those?" Lamé points at the machine.

With a muttered, "Dammit," I eye a fresh batch of arrivals. "Making coffee paid for books my first couple years of college." I don't bother mentioning that I never graduated. "I just don't usually deal with money." I glance nervously at a loud group that's just entered. "Or people."

Lamé apparently finds this hilarious. She claps her hands. "Listen up, guys!"

Her voice is remarkably effective at getting attention. "The lovely Grace here's gonna make your coffee, but she hates people."

"I wouldn't say I *hate* pe—"

"So, just accept her abuse like good little subs and give her a massive tip, because she's saving my ass today."

Someone says something about it being a fine ass and the crowd breaks out into laughter. A couple big bear-looking guys offer to help Lamé to the medical cabin. She's positively simpering when they pick her up. They're almost to the door when she has them turn her around, in the manner of an empress atop her litter. "Oh, Grace, honey."

I pause my frantic efforts to understand the coffee shop's system, and look up.

"You've got something on your neck."

My hand flies up to my shoulder. Sure enough, there's a faint swelling. Oh my God. My fingers tingle. It's where he bit me last night.

With a smirk, Lamé grand exits. If that's even a thing.

Shit.

"Nice bite."

Oh, God, I can't talk about this.

Ignoring the peanut gallery, I pour myself a filtered coffee and breathe deep.

I really don't feel comfortable talking to strangers. And it's not that I don't like them. It's that I lose my cool when I have to talk and do math and perform under pressure. Making coffee, pushing buttons on a machine, and holding a conversation all at once?

Especially a machine I've got no idea how to run? Nightmare.

Add in small talk and it's sheer torture.

My eyes lose focus and my hands go still halfway through tying on an apron. Oh my God. What if that's part of what I like about my nighttime escapades? We bypass all the awkward get to know you business and go straight for the good stuff.

"You all right?" I turn to face the crowd. The speaker is a middle-aged Black woman at the front of the line, in expensive gym clothes. She looks like she just left her hot yoga class. "We'll be nice. Promise."

"I won't bite," comes a deep voice from behind her.

"Unless you ask him to," someone else calls out. Everyone laughs.

Others join in. "Might have to beg."

"Nice apron."

I look down and break into giggles when I see that it's got enormous naked breasts printed on it. "Thanks." Humming nervously under my breath, I do a half circle, open a fridge, pull out milk, find the coffee beans, the grinder button. Okay. There's a wet rag here for cleaning the steamer. Cups are there. All to-go, which makes things easier. Muffins and donuts and cookies in the case. I can do this.

"Okay. What'll it be?"

"Triple shot half-caff caramel latte with a third almond milk, a third soy and... Nah. Just kidding." The woman grins. The motley crew behind her joins in. No one here seems rushed, so at least there's that. "I'll take a latte. Large. No bells or whistles."

The look I give her is relieved. "Thanks." I turn to make the drink and add a second, remembering poor Max back at the site, waiting for me. Probably worried by now. The woman, Jeanette—a spanking slut who has three partners, a dog, and a Sibian back home (and is possibly an over-sharer)—is happy to bring Max her coffee, especially since she'll be heading to the burlesque class immediately afterwards and is dying for a chance to chat with her first. I push some buttons on the screen, have her swipe her card, relieved when it goes through, and move on to the next drink and the next, fueling myself with sips of my own coffee when I can.

The minutes speed by. By the time I get my head out of the weeds, it's almost eleven, which I cannot believe. Bone-tired, I spray the counters and espresso machine, run a bar towel over everything, look over at the wall clock and catch sight of the message board, which I'd totally forgotten up until now.

Insides fizzing, I head over for a closer look.

19

Liev

I came straight back to my studio last night, where my hunk of granite called out like a long-lost siren.

I haven't slept. I've only hammered. I couldn't stop, not even to take a break. When it comes on like this—and it's been a hell of a long time—chipping away at a rock is a compulsion I can't deny, my hands and eyes and brain so focused on making, my other bodily functions cease to exist.

My eyelids are gritty, my calluses scraped raw, hands sore, arms putty. I need to piss, grab a coffee. I should probably eat. I need sleep, too, but first...

I have to check that damn message board.

I slug back a glass of water, refill it at the tap and down another. My body's dead tired, my muscles stiff slabs of rock, my bones hurting like they never used to when I was a young artist, pulling all-nighters for the fun of it. I set the glass down and it's smeared with dust. A look down shows my entire body in the same state. Shit.

Maybe I'll call Lamé, check in on things and just casually ask if there's anything new to report.

Before I can question myself too deeply, I grab my phone. Battery's in the red, but it should be enough.

I hit call and wait. No response. Impatient, I try again, this time on the landline instead of Lamé's mobile.

Immediately, someone answers. It's definitely not Lamé.

"Um, hello. This is the coffee shop. Uh, Camp Haven coffee shop, I mean." There's a rough edge to the voice that makes me think I'm dreaming.

"Who is this?" *And what is it about your voice that's made my cock half-hard?*

"Uh, this is Grace, filling in for Lamé. Who is *this?*"

"This is Liev." I shut my eyes and dig into them hard with my thumb and forefinger. I'm too tired to figure out if I'm imagining the similarity between this voice and my mystery woman's "Where's Lamé?"

"She hurt her ankle. Looked pretty bad, to be honest."

"Where are they now?" I push harder on my eyeballs, turning my vision into a kaleidoscope of bright shapes.

"Oh. They. Right. They went to see the medic. They're fine."

I'm already moving. "Was it the skates? It was the fuckin' skates, wasn't it?"

"Yeah." She laughs, the sound low and rough. I press the phone harder to my face. "Are you the one who said they'd put an eye out?"

"You mean the kill-joy who wants them to be careful for their own damn good? Yeah, that's me." When she laughs this time, my hand drops to my side and I just listen. Once she goes quiet, I ask, "They okay, though? I'm heading down there. You said they're getting it looked at?"

"Yes. Lamé called. It's a small sprain, according to the Doc. Nothing bad."

Why, I wonder, didn't Kris call me?

"Good. Maybe it'll keep them off the skates in the damn shop."

Another low chuckle flows through the phone, slow as molasses and twice as sweet. "I somehow doubt that."

"Yeah." We share a short silence. I look down and realize I've stopped walking. I'm just standing outside like a dick. "So, uh, you're working the coffee shop?"

"Just to help out, I mean, I won't take their tips or anything. It was crowded and—"

"We'll pay you." I look at the clock again. It's edging close to lunchtime. "You been there long?"

"Couple hours."

"Look. I'll find you a replacement, okay? Or, better yet, I'll come down there and help out."

The ache in my back tells me this is a terrible idea, but I ignore it. I should definitely make sure everything's okay. "Thanks again for helping. Seriously."

"You're welcome." There it is again, that scratch in her voice, like low notes you can barely hear. All the little hairs on the back of my neck stand at attention.

"You said your name's Grace?"

"Yeah."

"I've got to take care of a couple things up here, but I'll be down there soon, okay? You mind holding tight?"

"Right. Yeah. Sure. Bye, um…Liev."

I hang up, the sound of my name in that voice resonating straight to my prick.

Buzzing now, though my body's heavy with exhaustion, I drag myself around to the side of the building, strip, and hose all the shit off before heading into the house where I run up and take a warm shower. Without meaning to, I'm palming my cock, thinking of last night and the taste of my mystery woman. Is it Grace? My exhausted brain's layered that phone voice over all the smells and sounds and sights I've built in my head.

In my mind, she's begging for more, deeper, harder. I'm so drained I have to lean against the tile wall, but my hand's working fast, my arm tense with my very last dregs of strength, my fist somehow tight as a fucking vise, while my balls ache to spill on her, in her. Fill her up with my come. Christ, it's been so long. I hardly remember how it feels to come raw inside a woman. That colossal mistake of a moment lit me up in places I forgot I had. I want to suck in her smell, bite her all over, mark her again with my teeth. Cover her in semen.

I think of Grace's low laugh over the phone and put a face to her—it's the shower woman. The phone, the shower, the Dungeon, last night. They're all her. Strong arms, wide hips, long, taut waist, with the soft belly and the wiry pubic hair I want to bury my face in again. My mystery woman's words come back to me, in that other voice, more immediate, more real, although surely the phone adds more distance than the dark.

"Please," she begged as she came. *"Please, please, please."* And *"You're my first"*, I imagine Grace's phone voice saying into my ear, embarrassed and shy and happy. *"I want you."*

The memories are pure fuel, turning up the flame until I'm so close to coming I can taste it. I tighten my hand, twist high at the tip, stroke to the base. When I look down, my cock's a dark, angry red, stiff and glossy, the slit beading with pre-cum. I overlay the black-haired woman onto what happened last night, her wide mouth open around me, her dark eyes tearing up. Another quick tug, another, and I'm there, the orgasm blasting through me, quick and hot. I blink without seeing the come splashing the tiles and my feet, getting washed away by water.

It takes me a solid minute to come back to reality and then another two minutes to towel off my hair—which needs a cut—and get dressed. I add at least another minute rooting around in the back of my dresser drawer to find a shirt that's a little nicer than the rest. I mean, it's a T-shirt, like the others, but without discernible holes. Blaming Zed, I throw that on and head down to the coffee shop.

Grace

I put the phone down.

"The hell's got you smiling like something the cat just humped, honey?"

Lamé is standing silhouetted in the doorway, propped up on crutches, wearing an entirely new outfit from the one they had on earlier. This one is a flowing robe with kimono sleeves and slits up both legs, in a head-to-toe fuchsia that makes me wish I had sunglasses. Possibly the most impressive part is the crutches, which are entirely blinged out in matching crystals.

They're flanked by a beautiful young man wearing a tank top made of chain mail and very tight, shiny booty shorts.

Let it never be said that Lamé doesn't make an impressive entrance.

"Lamé!" I start forward and meet them halfway across the room. "How are you?"

"I'm grand, honey. I mean, the show must go on, right, Jonas?"

"Yes, Mistress," the young man says in a deep, resonant voice, his eyes glued to the floor.

"What had you smiling?" Lamé asks. "Come on. Out with it."

"What?"

"When we came in. You looked..." They flick their fingers at my face. "All dreamy about something. A certain kiss, perhaps?"

"Probably."

"Who was on the phone?"

Why don't I want to say? "Your boss."

"The Overlord?" Their eyes go comically wide. "And?"

It takes me a second to come up with a response. "He was just checking in, I think? I told him about your ankle. He thanked me." My smile edges in again, remembering the gruff warmth of his voice as he joked about Lamé, full of affection. "He's not old, is he? I mean, I think I've seen him a couple times and he seemed kind of, what? 30-something?"

"He's 33, baby." Their intense focus pushes me to explain.

"He joked about how you called him an old man. For the eyes out comment, you know? The skates? It was kind of funny and…" I flail, wishing I'd kept my mouth shut instead of blubbering on and giving the whole silly conversation more importance than it deserves.

Except I've got a hunch that he's my stranger. In which case, I guess I consider the call important.

"Liev is the Overlord, right?"

"He is." Lamé nods, watching me. "He's an old soul, honey. The body, though." They wink. "Good stuff happening under those rags he wears." Head at an angle, their eyes shine bright and expectant as a crow's. "You might already have noted."

"Huh, maybe." I turn to the counter. Honestly, though. What am I supposed to do here? Admit my suspicions? Pretend I'm clueless?

Lamé cackle, nearly losing their footing, which causes Jonas to swoop in and wrap a big arm around them. "Put me down there," they tell him, imperious as a queen. Once settled, complete with a beaded satin pillow Jonas produces from out of nowhere, Lamé turns back to me. "So, anyone give you trouble here?"

"Not at all." I head back to the counter and grab the tip jar. "This is yours."

"Hell no." They turn away, a toddler refusing dinner. "The money's for you."

"No way! You're injured. I just helped out. I'm not accepting your—"

"Take it or else."

"Lamé will hurt you," says Jonas, who clearly has experience in the matter.

With a sigh and an eyeroll, I grab the jar and stuff the cash and coins into my pockets. I'll just give it back to them next time they work.

"Looks like you raked in the tips. Must make good coffee."

"I do okay."

Lamé squints at me through a virtual forest of fake lashes. "What is it you do, outside of this place?"

"I paint houses."

Their eyes widen. "How butch."

"Thanks?"

Someone walks in. Lamé says hello and gets sucked into conversation, waxing dramatic about their epic fall.

Just as I'm about to return to the counter to make a coffee, Lamé stops me. "No, girl. Nah ah." They point at the man who walked them in. "Jonas, you're up. Get on back there. Do your hot coffee boy magic."

He scurries to do their bidding.

"Thank you again." Lamé opens their arms for a hug. "You are a jewel in my crown, honey. A jewel."

"I'm glad I could help." I let them drag me into their fragrant bust for a second before they push me gently away.

"Now go and get fucked or something."

I think of the way things ended last night. *Or something* seems more likely.

"Okay. Sure. On it. Bye Lam—" Laughing, I spin right through the door, where I smack straight, mid-twirl, into a big, hard wall. All the air gets knocked out of me, with an audible, "Oooof!"

Hands catch me around the waist before my feet get any more tangled up.

Dazed, I grab onto the wall, which isn't, in fact, a wall at all, but a chest. I've got one hand wound up in soft cotton, the other gripping hard muscle. For a few stunned seconds, I can do nothing but cling and work to get my breath back.

I unwind my hand from the fabric and rub my jaw. Along with my shoulder, it took the brunt of the hit. "Oh, ouch." I shut my eyes, waiting for my head to stop spinning. What is wrong with me?

"Don't move." The chest vibrates against mine.

"Okay." I sound weak, which is ridiculous. You don't get head trauma from bashing into people in doorways. I open my eyes and shut them again. "Uh oh."

Unless it's this megalith. Then it's possible there's head trauma.

The hands at my waist shift until I'm being held tight in two sturdy arms and, for a handful of seconds, I'm back under the trees in the dark.

I force my eyes open. Sky blue cotton, a peek of dark chest hair, a thick, angular collar bone framing a wide neck, the sides wrapped in tendons, Adam's apple textured with a dusting of rough-looking stubble that runs up to a square, immovable jaw—carved from stone. Above that, a tight-lipped mouth, a hefty nose, and faded-denim eyes that look somehow young and like they've seen too much. Above it all is dark brown hair I want to ruffle with my fingers.

Heat rushes my cheeks and I know for a fact that I'm blushing. It's the guy. The shower guy, the Dungeon guy. The man I kept picturing while humping my stranger to orgasm last night. The Overlord.

His features are spare, as if the years have taken their toll, only instead of adding the usual soft layers, they've weathered him down to sharp bones, deep dips, harsh angles. Time's sanded away the extraneous and left nothing but this unpolished version. Despite the thick muscles packed into his body, he seems pared down to the bare minimum. Bleak. That's how I'd describe him.

Bleak and so fucking beautiful.

I have no idea why he appeals to me so much, but he does. And not just to my eyes, but to my body, as well. It's responding to this man's embrace the way it did to my stranger's last night in the woods.

Maybe it's time to admit that he's one and the same.

It's a good thing he told me not to move, because I can't. I've got my hands on his shoulders and my boobs pressed flat up against him and he smells good.

Like really, *really* good. He smells like Lava soap and dust, the sun-warmed musk of skin.

Maybe I don't want to move.

And yeah, I know exactly who he is.

"It's *you*." I'd know him anywhere, could feel him from the other side of a crowded room. I'm a celestial body in his orbit.

He shakes his head.

My heart cracks. Or maybe that's just my feelings. Either way, I'm hurt.

"You okay?" Faint lines fan out from his eyes, around his mouth, on his forehead. None of them could possibly have come from smiling over the years.

Our gazes connect and it zaps me again, a hit of shock or fear, some prescient notion that everything's about to change. My insides are a mess of embarrassment and hurt. The timing's all wrong, but my pulse is spiking and my body's responding and what it wants me to do is *run*.

"I...I'm so sorry," I manage, tamping it all down for the sake of appearances. I sound breathy, though. I want to run and I want him to chase me and it's never quite come over me like this.

"Grace." It's not a question.

I can't help that it sends a thrill right through me, from my hard-as-nails nipples to the tips of my toes and back up to curl heavily between my legs. "Yeah?" Where'd all the oxygen go?

His head tilts at an angle, giving me a clearer view of crinkled eyes and brows like wings. His neck is thick, his shoulders massive. He isn't particularly tall—maybe a couple inches over my five foot eight—but height wouldn't matter to a man so firmly rooted in the ground.

Of *course* he didn't move when I crashed into him. He's not just made of stone, he probably sucks it straight from the earth's core, like a tree drinks water from the soil. This man, I've decided in the very short time I've been in his orbit, is unbreakable, steady, immovable as steel. And maybe just a little bit frightening.

"I'm Liev."

"Yeah." I know exactly who you are. "I figured."

"I would tell y'all to get a room." Lamé's voice cuts through the unearthly haze. "But, hell, it's Camp Haven. Go for it right here."

20

Liev

She extricates herself from my hold. Immediately, I miss her.

Grace.

I knew it.

Hell, that first look across the Dungeon, the way the air sizzled hotter. I knew it then.

Close up, she's absolutely breathtaking. I knew she would be.

She's tall and slender, dressed in a faded black T-shirt and jeans, with a face that's long, tragic—a soulful Modigliani, with freckles and two red flags flying high on her cheeks. She's so beautiful my heart hurts.

In the light of day, her features are shockingly mobile. Alive. I want to stare at her face, that mouth, those crushingly expressive eyes. Even her hair is electric somehow, the waves alive, almost dancing. I want to spear my fingers into the dark mass and tug.

The second her body ran into mine, mine woke back up. The moment our gazes met was *explosive*.

Now, something's happened in my chest that I swear is physical. Heartbeats finding a new rhythm.

"Thank you for your help, Grace." I sound robotic.

She gives a quick, puzzled smile. "Shouldn't I thank you?"

"I meant this morning. Here. At the coffee shop."

"Oh. Sure." A blush works its way up her chest, her neck, to darken her already rosy cheeks. "I hope I didn't screw up too badly."

"Of course not. I appreciate the way you jumped right in." I slide my hand into my back pocket and pull out a couple hundreds I grabbed before setting out.

She steps back, trapped between me and a table, and puts up her hands. "Oh, no. No, I can't take that."

I unglue my eyes from her callused palms to frown at the money, then back at her. "Why not?"

"It's Lamé's." Her hand makes a motion toward where Lamé sits at a corner table like a spider in their web, wearing a self-satisfied smile. Behind the counter is Lamé's sub-du-jour, Jonas, making coffee.

I give him a nod, which he returns with a subtle wink.

"Lamé will get paid, too. I wouldn't not pay someone because they got hurt on the job."

"That's not the point." Her blush goes impossibly darker.

"What is the point?"

"I don't want it." She appears to realize how harsh she sounded and tempers her words. "I just wanted to help."

"Understood." I nod. "Thanks again."

"I guess I'll, um, head out." With a lopsided smile, she steps towards me. I move to the side to let her pass, but she goes that way as well. I move right, then left again, each shift mirrored by her. This little shuffle's another dance.

I tilt my head a couple degrees, my eyes tracking her movements. I don't have to look down to see the quick rise and fall of her chest. I can feel it, just like I sense the vibration between us.

I swear if she were an animal, she'd be a gazelle or something, twitching with the awareness of prey the moment their senses detect a predator. My body gets bigger, hers goes completely still. These roles that feel ancient, carved in stone, forged from flesh and bone and blood.

For so long, I missed the thrill of *wanting*. And now it's all I've got.

The thrill of watching a woman squirm in bright daylight. A woman who wants to get caught, who smells like fear, which, in this case, is exactly like sex. Above all, though, I missed the rightness of this—desire and *need* and the knowledge that I can have it and when I get it, it'll be mine. A fight, but worth it.

The sex I've had these past few years felt flimsy. It was sex, yes, it was hunting, but nothing about it ever felt real. My partners and I were wraiths, not solid, flesh and blood beings. Not like this. Her.

I want her.

I shouldn't, though I'm no longer clear on why.

I should get out of her way, but I can't and it's not just that my dick's inexplicably hard, it's...something else.

"What are we doing here, Liev?" Grace asks, her voice scratchy and low, the timbre so rich I can feel it in my balls.

There are many ways to interpret that question, but I know what she means. Why bother pretending otherwise? "I don't fucking know." It's the truth. It's all I've got.

She sighs. "I should go." When I don't reply, she gives me a brittle smile. "See you around, Overlord."

"I prefer Liev."

Someone comes in from outside and stops short. "Oh, excuse me. Do you think I could get inside and grab—" Grace takes the opportunity to scoot around me. "Oh, my God, you're the Overlord, right?"

God, I hate that name. I hold back a sigh and force my expression into something approaching amicable. "So they tell me." Grace is walking away. "Grace. Hold on."

"Oh, wow. I've been wanting to thank you," the newcomer says. "For donating. To the cancer fund."

"Sure." I smile and nod. "Grace!"

She waves without turning. "I'll see you around, Overlord."

"It's Liev!" I yell at her departing back.

"Goodbye, Liev."

The other person's still talking. I do my best to engage with them, but all I can hear is that rough little voice as she walks away, leaving me raw and aching and wondering what the hell's happened to my insides.

It's not until she's just edging out of view that I see the red mark at the juncture of her shoulder and her neck.

My red mark. *Mine*.

The beast awakens inside me. It's a pathetic, wounded creature, snapping to get out.

My vision blurs. Fuck, I'm wasted.

"Sit your ass down, Liev," Lamé's voice cuts through the *whomp whomp* of blood pounding in my veins. I blink at a chair and sink into it, faster than I meant to. My strength's just gone.

Vaguely, I hear Lamé telling the customer that the Overlord's indisposed at the moment. The person gives me a wide berth as they scoot up to the coffee counter.

"Mm-mm-mm." Lamé swings over on their

crutches and settles in the seat beside me. I look up expecting one of their signature smirks, but all I see is fondness. And maybe a little pity. Or a lot.

"I'm fucking up."

Lamé—or Kris in this moment—throws their head back and laughs, the sound deep and rich. It brings back nights up at the house with Helen and Zion and a handful of other friends. Helen always at the center of it all, always playing, always joyous and open and full of life. So happy to spread it around—all that love she had in her heart.

Where the hell did it all go when she died?

Skin prickling hot and cold, I turn a wild look on Lamé. They're shaking their head, an affectionate smile on their face. "You've come a long way since Helen died, Liev. You may not see it yet, but you're not the guy we found drunk and half-starved in his studio."

I know this to be true, but there are still moments of guilt. Of feeling like I don't deserve whatever goodness comes my way.

"Cut yourself some slack."

"I just...shit, Lamé. I'm pretty fucking rusty at this." It comes out more snarl than actual language.

"Then listen to Lamé, old man. Step one." Leaning close, Lamé grips my chin in three long-nailed fingers. "Is wake up and smell the pussy."

I snort. The person waiting for their coffee doubles over with laughter.

"Fuck." I shake my head and look back the way

Grace went, fighting the urge to hunt her down and lick the bite mark on her neck. "I'm so tired, Kris. So damn tired."

"Step two: get your ass to bed."

I drop my head on one hand. "And then?"

"Then you go get your girl."

"That sounds backwards."

She flicks her fingers towards the door. "Go."

21

Grace

Okay. That happened.

I'm literally shaking as I walk down the path back to the Thunderdome, and not just because I haven't eaten a thing today—of which my stomach reminds me loudly.

Did it even happen? I mean all of it, from the fall, to the clench, to the weird-ass conversation, could have come straight from my fantasies. The Overlord. Liev, the Barbarian.

But my fantasy men were never real in my mind. They were amorphous. An idea. A desire.

That man is the opposite. He's...a rock. A solid mass. An impenetrable force.

Liev. I try out his name as a whisper. It's short and skates across my tongue. It's a good name and it suits him much better than Overlord, which is pretentious and kind of absurd and also remote. There's nothing remote about him. At all.

Shit. I've got to calm down, wrestle my libido into submission and get myself a damn snack. And maybe a shower.

That just makes me think of him again.

So, maybe a wank in that shower.

I look up to see the Thunderdome's striped awning just ahead, complete with rope swags and fairy lights. It looks like home. Relief sweeps through me with unexpected vehemence.

I just need to get back there and regroup, rest, refuel, and figure out just how I feel about this rabbit hole I've fallen into.

Dived into, more like. Head first.

At our campsite, I grab water and a bag of chips, then collapse onto the grass.

Lazy clouds float above. Seahorse. Rocket. Elephant. Why's there always an elephant?

The trees' bright green leaves don't move at all in the still heat. It is hot today, isn't it? I polish off the bottle and tear into the chips like a starving woman.

"Hey, hot stuff." A silhouette blocks out the sunlight. Once the first thrill passes and my eyes adjust, I recognize Zed. He's wearing board shorts and flip-flops, looking like he belongs in the sun, on the water, except for the mask covering most of his face. Today's mask is leather, with holes for breathing and straps buckled behind his head. It's less Batman and more steampunk.

Geez, even wearing that, he's really stunning.

"Hi," I say through a mouthful of chips.

"Hungry?"

"Why do you say that?" I snag another handful and scarf it down, then offer him the bag.

He hesitates. "Mind if I sit?" How very Kink Camp of him to ask. Gotta love the constant requests for consent.

"Be my guest."

He accepts the bag and settles onto the grass. After watching me for a time, he flops back to watch the sky from my angle. "How's camp treating you?"

"Good question."

"Uh oh."

"No, it's fine. Just…a lot."

"I've been coming for years and it's still overwhelming on occasion."

I turn toward him and catch my breath. Seriously. That's what he is: breathtaking. With the mask covering his mouth and nose and the rest of him mostly bare, he's mysterious and outlandish, like something from a comic book. I squint. Definitely a villain.

"Hang on." I don't stop to think before looking around for my pad and pencil.

Shit. Where'd I put them?

"Lose something?"

"I don't know."

"What are you looking for?"

"A little brown sketchpad. Black pencil." They're not on the trestle table or the lawn chairs or anywhere else. I check the tent. "Dammit." It takes me a minute to a remember that I've got a small notepad in my bag, along with a pen. It's better than nothing, I guess, since the compulsion to draw's not letting up.

Still a little worried that I've somehow lost my pad, I grab the replacement, unearth a tablet of chocolate from our supplies, and settle into a folding chair.

Zed rolls onto his side, leans his head on his hand and watches me, which would be unnerving if I weren't about to do the exact same to him. "You're an artist, huh?"

"No." My answer's low and definitive. "It's just a hobby."

His lush lips compress the tiniest bit into an expression of disbelief. "Are you drawing me?" His thick lashes flicker with every stroke of my pencil. In this light, his eyes are a saturated green. They look fake.

I nod. "Is that your real eye color?"

"Wouldn't you like to know?"

I laugh. "You're kind of ridiculous, aren't you, Zed?"

"I don't know. Is ridiculous your thing, Grace?" He lifts one perfectly-shaped eyebrow. "Does it turn you on?"

Still laughing, I sketch horns onto his head, eye the drawing and then flip the page to start a new one.

"So..." Apparently unperturbed by my lack of an answer, he asks, "Can I move?" At my nod, he stretches, the muscles straining and bunching with the grace of flowing water. "You know, seeing as how you're a first-timer. I was thinking back to my first camp. I had to be sat down and given a talking to."

"A talking to? Why?"

He blows a lazy raspberry, the sound muted by the thick leather. "I was such a prick. Shoulda been kicked out on the spot."

"Ouch. What'd you do?"

"Butted in on someone's scene. Tried to tell a guy his knots were crap." His cheeks go high and round, making his eyes look impish. "Turns out he was literally the country's best rope man. He took it in stride. The boss man did not."

My pulse kicks up. "The Overlord?"

"Yeah." My curiosity couldn't be more piqued, but I keep my mouth shut, flip the page, and start another sketch, my hands moving before my brain recognizes the intention.

"We weren't friends back then. He and his wife had just bought the place."

My stomach clenches, hard. His wife? Oh, shit. For a second there, I was into a married man. I know all about polyamory, given Max and her multiple partners. Primary partners, secondary partners, play partners. Then the partners' partners. It's a mixed up ball of yarn that's way too complicated for me.

Disappointment's a lump in my throat.

"He was not impressed." At my eyebrow raise, his smile deepens. "Bastard was scary."

"So what happened?"

"He told me to fix my ways or I was out—for life." He arches back into a stretch that's so pretty, he's surely doing it on purpose. "I groveled. And I got the hots for him—and the wife. They were really important to me. Helped me through some tough times." He does another slow stretch, as languid as a cat in the sun. "I sort of forced him to become friends with me." His eyes crinkle and I'll bet there's an evil grin under that mask. "Poor guy'll never get rid of me now."

Still a little wounded by the mention of Liev's wife, I force out a laugh. Zed smiles, working hard to charm me. For what feels like ages, we loll in the sun, smelling the grass and the chlorine from the pool, with the light music of laughter and conversation all around us. It's an easy silence and, though he's clearly a flirt, I feel safe and calm with him. It doesn't hurt that he's a pleasure to draw.

After a while, he lowers his chin towards my pad. "You got a card or something?"

"What?"

"For the artwork. You're really good."

"Oh. No. It's just doodling."

"I try not to ask too many questions at camp,

but..." One finely-muscled shoulder lifts. He leans in, takes a slow, sultry breath and whispers, "I don't mind breaking my own rules."

His eyes are pretty. His body's...wow. And he's trying, like, really, really hard, which I appreciate. And, yet, I feel nothing. I check in with my various parts. Not a flicker of interest.

"For example, I can tell you that I'm a very, very famous person." He looks left and right, as if setting up a joke, or hiding from a crowd. "Deep under cover." He shows me the bright yellow band on his wrist. No pictures, it means.

"Is that so?" Smiling, I start a new sketch, this time hinting at the nose he keeps hidden and the mouth I saw briefly a couple nights ago. If I can put the pieces together...

"Okay... Lemme guess what you do in real life." His eyes glimmer as he leans back, probably purposely flexing his six pack, and looks me up and down. "You're a mountain climber."

"What?" I giggle. "No."

"Supermodel."

"Shut up."

"Landscaper."

"Uh uh. Although that's remarkably close."

"Lawn waterer?"

"That's called a sprinkler. And it's not a job. It's a thing."

He throws up his hands, palms out, in a sort of easy, charming, tall guy mea culpa. I mean, I enjoy that he's funny and flirty and that I've got interesting company in the midst of all this debauchery and my own inner heartache, but seriously. Not a flutter.

"I paint houses," I finally tell him, my stomach already tightening at the prospect of going back to work on Monday.

"Whoa." He leans back and examines me. "Sexy."

I lean down and smack him with my pad and he catches it. I dive for it and wind up on the ground, half on top of him. He's hot and smells like sun on skin and sweat. Suddenly, he goes still, his eyes hard and watchful. My breath rattles in my lungs.

"Ohhhhh. This what you like?" he whispers. "To be taken down?" His eyes go wide. "Shit. It is, isn't it?"

"Maybe." I swallow.

His sharp gaze does a circuit of my face, lingering on my lips before returning to look straight in my eyes. "You sure you're not into cocky, pansexual sadists with godlike bodies and charming personalities?"

"A sadist, huh?"

"Yep." He winks.

When he doesn't go on, my curiosity gets the best of me. "So, like, you want to spank people? Or whip them or whatever?"

"Depends."

"On what?"

"Circumstances. Where and when and who I'm

playing with. Someone like you, for example? All tragic eyes and sinful mouth, with those long, long legs..." His head falls lazily to one side, but the stone cold look in his eyes is pure tension. "I'd reserve the big stage, in the main Dungeon."

My mind goes right there—to the massive, permanent structure built at one end of the big gymnasium. Unconsciously, my stomach muscles clench, as if my imagination's slid me straight into the scene.

22

Liev

There's a lightness in my step as I make my way past the pool and a group of cabins towards one of the tenter areas. It's ridiculous, I know, but when Jonas found the pad and pencil behind the counter, giving me an excuse to go after Grace, it felt like fate intervened. As if maybe being happy is allowed. As if she left her stuff there on purpose, giving me an excuse to find her.

Lamé warned me that it was perhaps unwise to race off after a woman in my current state, but a double espresso helped. Now, I'm just excited.

On the hill to my right, the pony enclosure's overflowing. It's clearly a meetup or some special event.

It's also possible that I just haven't noticed the uptick in ponies this year. Up ahead, the tents are gathered into little clusters that always remind me of Smurf villages. The first village is crowded with campers. A young Black couple plays cards at a folding table, chatting with a retired gay couple who've been coming to camp since the beginning.

They wave hello as I walk by and I wave back. Across from them, a woman sits casually on another woman's face. She smiles and waves. Feeling a little more a part of things than I have in a while, I wave back, then pick up my pace as I near the area where Lamé told me I'd find the campsite apparently referred to as the Thunderdome. According to Lamé, I should have known about the Thunderdome, and Mad Max, the woman who occupies it every summer. Grace's best friend.

Been a little busy, I told Lamé, although it does seem suddenly as if maybe I should pay more attention to what's happening down here. Maybe, I concede for the first time, Lamé's not all wrong when they call me the Grinch. Because, yeah, the camp's mine, but aside from the occasional emergency intervention here and there, I spent a three full seasons essentially ignoring it.

I had work to do. It's true. The commissions have ramped up over the years, in price, if not quantity. I'm down to one or two sculptures a year for which I'm paid very well.

Weirdly, that feels a lot like an excuse.

The real reason I don't come down anymore has more to do with what drew me here to begin with—and that was Helen. As always, stirring up memories hurts, pushing out these unfamiliar good feelings, and bringing back the last year of her life. A year of pain, guilt. A year of begging and praying. A year of losing all faith. In everything.

There's another thing, though, something deeper and more confusing. The camp doesn't feel like it's mine. It feels like it's everyone's. So coming down under the guise of some overlord, benevolent or otherwise, doesn't sit well with me.

Someone screeches in the distance and a much older memory washes through me, from the good days, when I was Helen's person and she was mine.

It's sunny today just like the first time I saw her at my neighbor's Fourth of July picnic. It smelled like cut grass and grilled meat. Kids played soccer in the big field behind their house and she was there with them—tiny and round, smiley and soft-looking. She was terrible at playing sports. All of them, I found out later on. At one point, she got the ball and started dribbling down the field, a bunch of kids after her. Rather than go for the goal, she freaked out and raced in my direction, laughing and shrieking, as if running for cover.

I'll never forget how she threw herself into my arms. Not hesitating for a second, I dropped my beer and caught her. That was it for me. I was a goner.

Fuck, she was cute. My kinky little brat. The lifestyle wasn't even on my radar when we met, but she schooled me pretty damn quick. I eventually became her Dom, although it wasn't ever a role that fit me perfectly. And somewhere along the way, my inner beast came out. A Primal who could be a Dom. A sub with brattish tendencies. It worked. We made it work.

Someone runs across the path right in front of me, chased by a second person, who apparently recognizes me, and comes to a full stop, eyes open wide, as if... Fuck. Like I am the damn Grinch who's finally made it down to Whoville.

Lamé's right—I need to get involved again or I need to sell up and get out.

Selling, though, would mean losing not just Helen's dream, but my people. My family.

I can't do it.

"Hello!" I force out in an over-friendly voice, like I can compensate for three years of absence in one jaunty greeting.

"Hey, man," the guy replies. Oh, shit. I know him. It's... "Sledge," he tells me. "We used to..."

...*be friends*. Dammit, I'm an asshole.

But also, he used to fuck my wife.

I work my face into a smile. "Yeah, man. Good to see you." My hand lifts in an awkward wave. "See you around."

"Sure." He grins and takes off after whoever he was chasing. One of his partners. I have no idea who he's with now. Three years. That's how long it's been since I've had a relationship other than with my two very close friendships.

Running into her earlier—Grace—was weirdly like that first meeting with Helen. Except, instead of jumping into my arms like an excited little fairy, Grace smacked into me as if thrown by fate.

I glance down at the sketchbook in my hand, suddenly nervous. Just returning something, man. That's all. There's nothing fateful about it. Nothing to get superstitious about.

A little jittery now that I've put pressure on this thing, I round the last bend. Her spot's to the right, behind some trees. I hear voices murmuring, low and intimate. A man laughs, then a woman joins in.

Words pop out of the mumbling, random at first, then coming together to make sense.

"Beat the shit out of you, in front of everybody." That's Zion. I'd know his voice anywhere. "Stretch those hard little nipples out till you screamed. Choke you just enough to make you dizzy and wanting, then wreck your pussy with my massive cock."

I see them now. She's half on top of him and he's got an arm around her waist. I want to fucking howl at the way he's holding her—as if she belongs there.

I don't move, though my body tenses up.

My wiring's short-circuited, synapses blowing, nothing moves.

"...make you come so hard it hurts, but you want that. You want the pain and humiliation." The asshole's so goddamn confident. Of course she wants him. The words flicker in and out. Is it his voice wavering or my mind? "...stretch you wide open... other people...hungry little slut... Make you come... beg for more."

I don't hear her answer. Don't want to see what happens next.

My only choice is to get out of here. Now.

Gripping the notebook, I take off.

GRACE

"No, thank you," I tell Zed, moving off him before he tries to actually pull any of that stuff. "I most definitely do not want that." The whole thing's destabilized me, if I'm being honest.

"You sure?"

"A hundred percent." I feel almost like a liar.

With a regretful sigh, he hands over my pad. "Oh, well."

Breathing unsteady, I focus hard on my drawing, slash pen to paper, crosshatching a deeper shadow. Why? Why do I want what he described, and yet...I really, really don't?

Make you come, begging for more.

I don't want it with Zed.

Liev, however... I'd crawl in the dirt for another

chance with him. I'd beg him to make me come, any way he wants.

I force my breathing to steady. Married. Taken. Unavailable. I want to ask Zed about that, but don't dare.

His eyes narrow. "God, though. That voice of yours. How'd it get all scratchy like that?" His volume drops. "Bet it cuts in and out when you scream, doesn't it?"

Embarrassed heat sears everything from my chest to my face and I can't help sounding annoyed. "Can we stop now?"

"Oh. Sure. Yep. Absolutely. Apologies. I just..." He tilts his head. "You're hard to suss out. I'm too curious for my own good, I guess." Curious? Is that what it is? His eyes crinkle into another charming smile. "I love a mystery as much as I hate not knowing something."

My pen slows and finally comes to a stop. I lift it before it makes a splotch on the paper. I've opened up a lot here, I've said things I'd never have uttered in the outside world. I've looked people in the eye and released information I've barely even admitted to myself for most of my life.

After everything I've done in the past few days, saying it should be easy, right?

I swallow. "I like to be..." I clear my throat. Shit, dude. Just spit it out. "I'm into Primal kink. Like, running away. I'm the Prey." My breathing eases, my chest relaxes. "I've been playing with someone here."

"Yeah? How was it?"

How was it? Geez, Zed. Asking the big questions here. It was...

In the end, it was everything. And more.

Slowly, I break into a huge smile, which his eyes immediately mirror. "It was beyond my wildest dreams. So much better."

He puts out his hand and, laughing, I slap the palm. "Whoa." His warm, dry fingers wrap around mine. "What's this?"

I pull away, tightening my fingers into a fist to hide the rosebud in the center of my palm. "Just part of my tattoo."

"Holy shit. Wow, Grace. Who did it? I mean, the piece on your arm's gorgeous, but this is some of the best work I've ever seen."

"Thanks."

"You get this done around here?"

I shake my head, shyly pleased at the compliment.

"Wait. You did it?"

I look down at my palm. "Yeah."

"On yourself?" He sucks in a deep, audible breath. "That is *fierce*, woman. I don't know how good you are at painting houses, but you should be inking people." He watches me. "You are bad ass."

I can't quite hold my smile in.

"So, the Primal play," he says casually. "Was it, like an...anonymous thing?"

"Yeah. I never saw him, while we...did it. I just

answered an ad." Holy shit. Has it just been three days? "It was..." A slew of adjectives race through my brain, but none seem right for what happened.

"Beyond your wildest dreams?" He repeats from a minute ago, looking up at the sky.

"Yeah. And way better than the fantasy."

He looks at me, his eyes more serious than I've seen them. "That doesn't happen often."

"It was planned as a one-time thing, you know. Except we went back... Then last night..." I shut my eyes.

"You okay?"

"Yeah. No. I don't want it to be over, I guess."

"You sure it's over?"

My hand unconsciously rubs the stem tattooed from my heart, down my left arm, its thorns a warning. I stare down at the plump little rosebud inked into my hand. It's my secret. My arm's what I give the rest of the world, but the rosebud's the tender little heart of me.

I knew it would hurt.

"It's over." There. Now it's final.

Zed hums. "So... Last night? Night before?" he prods gently, head tilted.

My eyes meet his. "The last three nights." My pencil pauses. "Why?"

"No reason. No reason at all." With that, he gets up with a slow, showy stretch. "Sorry to love you and leave you, my dear, but all this talk's got me riled up. I'm off to find someone to play with."

"Okay. Have fun."

"Oh, hey. Let me get you coffee or something tomorrow."

I narrow my eyes. "Why?"

He puts a hand to his heart, his eyes wide and innocent. "Why? Must I have a reason to want to spoil a lovely new friend?"

"I just...feel like maybe there's something I'm missing here. Like, what are you getting out of this?" I wave my hand between us.

"Okay. Fine. There is an ulterior motive." He drops the wide-eyed look with a laugh. "I just figured I'd better start buttering you up now if I want you to ink me at some point." When I open my mouth to protest, he talks right through me. "I'll come get you at nine." He spins, then spins back. "Might want to cover that up." He lowers his chin towards the bite on my neck. "Unless you're good with people thinking you're taken."

With that, he grins, gives me a courtly bow, and jogs off, leaving me feeling pleasantly manipulated. Of its own volition, my hand seeks out the mark my stranger left on my neck.

I don't want to cover it up any more than my thorns. I want to show it off to the world.

23

L iev

I WAKE up from my nap, roll off the studio sofa, put on a record, and go right to work, diving into the soothing clang of hammer to chisel, the raucous bass of vintage heavy metal.

A metal mood, Helen used to call it. She'd stay away for as long as it took to beat it out of my system.

My metal moods scared her, she admitted once. They scared me, too. Reminded me of the way I felt when my parents argued. Like hitting things. Like wreaking havoc.

Except, as Bob my therapist pointed out, I destroy to create.

I haven't hated myself quite as much since I

started seeing Bob. I have Kris and Zion to thank for that.

Zion. Guts roiling, I throw up the mask, head over to the sink, and shove my head under the cold water.

Kris and Zion saved my life. No doubt about it. They showed up out of the blue a few weeks after Helen was gone to find me passed out, half-naked, and bleeding on the porch. I hadn't worked in ages, hadn't touched a chisel or a slab of stone. I'd barely eaten, hadn't bothered paying the bills, which led to the power getting cut off. My phone didn't work. And here I was, artist of the fucking year, with commissions out the ass, sitting on a goddamn pile of money big enough to buy the house and camp and whatever the fuck I wanted a dozen times over.

Couldn't buy Helen back to life, though. So, I drank and stewed in my hot metal mood until every vein felt lead-filled and vile. I wanted to die.

When they found me, I was pretty fucking close.

My knuckles were mush, I remember, from taking my agony out on my own self-portrait. What a sad prick.

I stop now and step back, breathe deep just to make sure I'm doing the things humans are meant to, and force myself to get a glass of water.

Seeing Zion flirt with Grace didn't just prod at my jealous streak, it reminded me that I'm not...

I'm not...

Fuck. My fist's already tight, aching to destroy

something. My chest's heaving. In search of something, anything, I turn and catch sight of the new sculpture and immediately remember the crunch of bone against hard rock, the split-second delay before the pain kicked in, the soul-deep frustration that no matter how hard I hit, I'd always be more friable than the stone.

My eyes focus down on the messy pile of granite chips littering floor. When my friends showed up, I was in pieces, just like that. A useless jumble of minerals.

Whereas now...

The door flies open.

I turn to see Zion saunter in and a mixed up rush of affection and pain sweeps through me. "Can't you knock?" I yell over the pounding music. He probably can't even hear.

He yanks off today's mask and throws it, missing the table, before collapsing onto the sofa, as if he's the one who's been pounding rock all day. As if he's the one rearranging his own insides.

He's red and sweaty and I suddenly don't want to know who he's been with. That jealousy thing rears up and, rather than face him—or it—I slam my own mask back over my face, grab my hammer, and set back to work.

After a few minutes, he shouts words that are stolen by the music, then finally gets up to shut it off, which leaves the two of us with nothing but the echo of hammer and chisel between us.

"You're gonna damage your ears, man."

"Who cares?" I feel petty and bratty as soon as the words are out. Ten-year-old Liev blasting music in my room so I didn't have to hear my parents arguing, again.

"What's up your ass? Aren't you getting laid these days?"

"Just once," I say, though immediately I want that to change.

"Thought it was twice?" he asks, casually.

"We, um, played three times." I go to the fridge and pull out a beer, not giving a shit what time it is. At Zion's nod, I grab him one, too. "Second time, I made her sit on my face." The sense memory of consuming her overtakes me. I press both cans to my hot skin, then hand his to Zion.

"I remember. Fuck, your woman smelled good. If I were you, I'd definitely go back for—"

"Quit it." Doesn't he know he held her in his arms just this afternoon? Gritting my teeth, I pick up a hammer and weigh it my palm. "Do anything fun today, Z?"

He rolls up to sitting, his muscles stretching and popping like he's just had a work out. Bastard probably has. "Tied up this pretty young chick named..."

Don't say Grace.

"Poppy something? Her partner, too."

Relief floods through me, warm and easy. "Thought I saw you with someone else."

"Oh, yeah?" His eyes lose their lazy glaze. "Huh. When was that?"

I should stop now, because I know if he figures out that I'm interested, he'll make life impossible. Kris already knows. The two of them together are like piranha when they smell blood. I'll never hear the end of it. "Just walked through one of the tenter areas. Saw you lounging with...someone I met."

"Hmmm." He throws his head back and appears to rack his brain, but the way he's acting... I've got that tingly feeling again. "Was it Ginny? You know, the little sub who gets off on sloppy face fucks? I hung out with her for a second. Or, maybe the Perkins? I caught them over by the drinks tent, with—"

My patience shatters. "I'm talking about Grace. She's tall, dark hair, thorns inked down her—"

"I know who Grace is." There is not an ounce of surprise on Zion's face as he watches me over the rim of his beer.

"Asshole."

"Sure am." One side of his mouth lifts in the signature grin that fans mistakenly find cute. The man is a shark. "What's that?" Zion points at my face. He looks worried.

"What?" I swipe at my cheek. "I get it off?"

"Nope. Here." He leans forward and clasps my face in his hand, the move reminding me of his first night here."That. Right there."

"Come on. What are you talking about?"

"Is that...it can't be. Is that an actual *smile* on your face?"

I pull away, half-annoyed. But only half. After another sip, I work up the courage to ask. "You got plans to play with her?"

"No, Liev. Why would I?" His eyes narrow on me. "When she's so clearly yours."

Blinking fast, I finish my beer, shake myself off, and make a decision. "I gotta go."

"Yeah?" Zion rolls to standing, smooth as a dancer. "Where to? You got a date?"

I shake my head. "Need a walk."

"Sounds good." He sinks back down, his all-knowing smirk pissing me off, and palms his dick. "I might just sit here and jerk off looking at the new sculpture, man. That's definitely the hottest thing I've seen you—" I stomp over to the shelves, grab a drop cloth, and throw it over the work in question. "Aw, come on, you cock-blocking son of a bitch."

"Make your own damn sculpture," I say, heading towards the door.

Zion, who usually laughs, calls out. "Forgot something."

I glance back to see Grace's sketchbook in his hand. It's been hell ignoring it all afternoon and, like an arrow to the heart, Zion goes straight for it. "Where'd you get this?"

"Grace left it at the coffee shop. I tried to return it, but you were—" He opens it, which feels like a violation, even to me. "Hey, man, you can't look at an artist's—"

"Whoa," he whispers.

I stop.

"You see these, Liev?"

There's no point answering now that he's opened Pandora's box.

"It's you, bro."

Me? I shake my head hard, like a dog, not quite getting why my eyes are so blurred.

"Look." He holds it open to one of the first pages. It's us. Her and me. She's against a tree, head thrown back, and I'm on her. I'm huge, my body made of boulders instead of flesh and hers is a mass of thorny vines, growing over me. Holding me up. Shit, the picture makes me hard and fucking terrified all at once, like she's somehow seen inside my soul and what she sees doesn't scare her.

The next one's me between her legs—a parched man drinking from her body. There are pages and pages of us, then others—in the Dungeon, I assume, but then—

I stagger back and topple onto the couch, boneless. "Wow," I mutter, blown wide open. Seen.

She drew me—face and all—two nights ago, in the Dungeon. No way she knew who I was then, right? And yet, I saw her that night, too, didn't I? There was recognition between us. I can't deny it.

In the picture, I'm a wolf, standing guard in a sea of sheep. My face remote, my body immoveable.

She's drawn me as a wolf made of *stone*, which is somehow the part that cuts deepest. I feel made of stone sometimes. She saw that. That very first day, she saw it from across the room.

Fingers numb, I flip through the remaining pages. There's a series of sketches of the sculptures I've got strewn around the property, which feels important, though I can't explain why. Lamé is there, too, at the end, a playful, benevolent Greek goddess on skates. I can't help but laugh.

"Pretty sure she likes you, bro."

I give Zion an annoyed glance, which he completely ignores.

"What are you gonna do?"

I flip the book closed, my brain already listing the reasons it's a bad idea.

"You know, Liev, Helen would want this."

"I know." I look at him head-on, my jaw hard. "Helen would be just fine sharing me with someone else. She'd have fucked *you* if you'd gone for it."

His eyes go soft the way they were all the time back when I leaned on him, just to function. "I knew you didn't share, Liev. Our friendship meant more to me than a roll in the hay with your wife."

"I loved her, man. I...I still love her."

"I know." He moves in close and bumps his shoulder to mine. "We all know."

"I let her go. I did. It was hard, but I got rid of her stuff, you know? Her clothes and crap. That felt...impossible."

He nods, uncharacteristically quiet.

"But *this*. The thing with Grace? It feels bigger. It feels like...the end."

"Or the beginning?"

I manage a strangled sound.

"Yeah. You like her." Zion smiles. It's an uncomplicated expression.

"Do I even know her?"

"Do you?"

I think of the way it felt to sit beside her in the woods. Just that, without the sex that brought us together. Shoulder to shoulder against the tree. "It feels right. That's all I know."

He taps the sketchbook with one long, manicured finger. "Don't waste this." Zion laughs soundlessly. "Helen would be so fucking pissed."

He's right. I never thought I'd feel this again, this rightness in my chest. And Helen, of all people, would push me to pursue it. She always did, whether I wanted to or not.

The air flowing through me is different, all of a sudden. Lighter, easier to take in, when breathing's been torture since she died.

The torture now is having to find Grace before I can have her.

Then again, there's nothing I love more in this world than a good hunt.

Grace

We're seated at a long table full of Max's friends.

We've got the Perkins: two extremely handsome men, who at camp never separate and are apparently known collectively as the Perkins. As in, together, they make a whole Perkins. Separate...I don't even know. They're wearing what I can only describe as designer loincloths. One is a very light-skinned Black man, with bright hazel eyes, while the shorter Perkins is so pale his skin's almost pearlescent white. They're two of the most beautiful people I've ever looked at; all energy and light, with a few well-placed muscles thrown in for good measure. They look happy. Not wide-grinning, fake happy, but deeply, truly content. I wonder if they'd mind if I drew them.

"Anyone going to Nasty Fest tonight?" one of them asks.

"I am," sings Max who, this trip has made me realize, is up for pretty much anything.

After they've all responded, they stare at me. I stare back, then realize there's a question I'm supposed to be answering. I turn to Max. "Do I even want to know?"

"Nope." She smiles.

"Awwww, cute baby camper," says the shorter Perkins. Perkin? "How much you wanna bet next year, you're back and you're like, teaching workshops?"

"I doubt it." I'm bright red now, of course.

"What's your plan for tonight then?" asks Pam, the sixty-something woman in leather bondage gear, wearing glasses on a chain like my grandma used to do. With her steel-grey bob and her sweet, round, red-cheeked face, this woman wouldn't look amiss in a library. Or darning Santa's socks at the North Pole. Of course, here, she's got her boobs hiked up almost to her chin and a leather collar around her neck, not to mention a life partner named Butch, who's the perfect central casting motorcycle gang dude, complete with the handlebar 'stache and tats and leather vest.

"Um. I might just...take it easy. Hang out at the campsite." Stay the hell out of the woods.

Butch gives me a kind look. "What is this for you? Day three?"

"Day four."

Everyone at the table says, "Fourth day slump."

"Gotta push through it," says a Perkins.

"Definitely take it easy," Max says from her spot beside me. "I want you to last all week."

"Thinking about leaving early?"

I shrug. "I've kind of accomplished what I came here to do."

Pam and Butch nod, as if they get it. The Perkins,

however, eye me with bright curiosity. "D'you get beaten?" asks one with obvious relish.

"Wait, wait, wait. Um..." The other closes his eyes. "Gangbang."

"No." I shake my head, half-laughing, and spoon chocolate mousse into my mouth.

A Perkins leans back to eye my butt. "Not a pet."

"Littles camp?"

I'm shaking my head, trying not to spit out my mousse, while they throw things out one after another.

"Fire?"

"Hooks!"

"Kidnapping?"

My heart sort of skips at that one, though I finally get the mousse down. "No!"

"Ropes? Wax? Whips?"

"No!" Max yells, getting into the fun. "Not even close! You guys aren't even warm."

"She's a Domme. I'm sure of it." The Perkins are both so into the game, they're jumping up to yell out guesses.

"Way into impact play! Right? Right? Am I right? I am, aren't I?"

I'm laughing so hard now I'm almost crying, which feels good. So, so good. Beside me, Max is doing the same. She slaps my leg with every wrong guess.

At some point, they'll hit on it.

Maybe.

"A voyeur. Just a garden-variety voyeur."

"Leather slut."

"Come slut."

"A doll!"

"Primal play."

I stop laughing. Max, too.

All eyes land on me, wide and happy.

"I guessed that," says one proud Perkins.

"You did, baby. You got it right."

The happy Perkins nudges me with his elbow. "You know if there's a Big Hunt this year?"

What? I blink the tears of laughter from my eyes, my body pricks up with interest.

"Ooooh, I love the hunt!" says Pam who, now that I think about it, is the carbon copy of Ms. Tancaredo, my middle school librarian. I can see her telling us to stop whispering in the stacks. "I do it every year."

I set my spoon carefully down and listen.

"It is so fun!" The Perkins say in perfect unison. I swear, these two should take their act on the road. The look they exchange is deliciously lascivious.

"What's, um..." I clear my throat, attempting a nonchalance I don't feel, and concentrating on Pam the librarian. "The Big Hunt?"

"Absolute mayhem," she replies with the kind of delight Ms. T. would have shown if asked a particularly challenging reference question, or when a kid developed a newfound love for reading.

Butch slides his arm over her shoulders. "My Pammie loves to run in the wild.

"Not to mention a good forced fantasy," she adds, her smile beatific.

My scalp prickles and I'm filled with a familiar rush.

"Oh, Pamela, honey," says the pale Perkins with what I can only describe as a guffaw. "We've heard you screaming..."

"For miles," the other finishes.

"What can I say?" Pam's blunt grey bob swings as she does a little shimmy. Her twinkling eyes meet mine. "I'm just a whore for violence."

"Not to mention a big, fat cock," her partner adds, his grin wide open, almost innocent.

"Or three!" squeal the Perkins, in unison.

"Is it happening this year?" Max asks the group. "I thought the Overlord stopped doing those."

My interest is beyond piqued.

"He was the king, wasn't he, back in the day?" A Perkins looks around the group.

"So sad," says the other Perkins, shaking his head. "The apex predator, taken down by love."

My stomach swishes unpleasantly and I push my bowl of mousse away.

"He'd bag more Prey than any others, wouldn't he?"

"Always," Pam says, sounding dreamy.

"Only ever fucked the wife, though."

"So, he's married?" I try my best to sound casual.

"He's a widower. She died."

My stomach sinks to my feet, the weird jealousy I'd felt morphing into shame. I know how loss feels. I wouldn't wish that on anyone.

"Yeah." Butch tightens his arm around Pam and pulls her in to kiss the top of her head. "Terrible, terrible thing."

I don't ask what happened. I don't want to know.

After a long silence, punctuated by the din of chatting and music and laughter from the other tables, one of the Perkins leans in, his lips pursed, his eyes narrowed. "You know what, though? He's around more this year. I saw him twice today."

"Right? Last night, too. The Masquerade? He was there." The Perkins nod, looking at each of us in turn.

"And the Dungeon!"

"It's been like, years, since he even went to a Dungeon night."

"Wonder if he's back in the game."

"That would make the ladies happy."

"One lady, at least." corrects Butch.

The Perkins both snort. One says, "The man could have as many as he wants."

"Overlord's a one-woman guy," Butch says, dead certain of what he's saying. "I imagine he always will be."

"Isn't it just tragic?" Pam looks like she might cry.

Butch, who's older and surer and looks like he has

more history in one little finger than me and the Perkins combined, nods. "Sure is."

Damn my stupid heart.

Abruptly, the hum of conversation and the dull clatter of cutlery and plates quiets.

We all look at each other.

"What's going on?" Max asks, while the Perkins crane their necks for a view of whatever's got people whispering.

"By the door." Pam's mouth drops open. "Oh, my goodness."

Butch turns to look, his eyebrows skyrocketing almost comically high. "Speak of the devil."

24

Grace

My lungs and my heart and my stomach do a little jig. I really wish I hadn't eaten the mousse.

On a deep inhalation, I turn and look, then immediately face front again.

Yep. Sure enough, it's Liev.

The Overlord has descended amongst his citizens. It's a big deal, apparently. The way everybody's acting, you'd think he was the Dalai Lama.

"Ouuuuff, I'd forgotten how hot he is," says Pam, fanning herself.

"What do you guys think he's doing here?" a Perkins asks.

Butch and I are the only ones not craning our

necks to see. He's busy eating and watching me with a funny look on his face. I'm sitting here feeling weirdly hot, buzzing with energy.

It doesn't take long for the big room's volume to rise back to normal. I guess the Overlord would have to do something pretty huge to keep this group's attention for long.

After a bit, I glance up and there he is. Just the sight of him makes me fluttery again. Or sick. Or fluttery. I don't know.

It affects me.

He and Zed look like they're searching the room. Someone by the door points in our direction. He turns, catches me staring, and starts moving.

Oh my God. What's happening here?

I can't breathe. Or maybe I can, I just don't feel it anymore.

The tone around us changes again. I barely notice. All I can do is watch his progress as he winds his way towards us—towards me—a leopard on the prowl.

I don't remember standing, though my chair makes a noise that stops everyone mid-sentence.

It's so quiet, you could hear a flogger drop to the tile floor.

By the time he reaches me, I'm functioning again, only now every breath takes a shuddering, labored effort.

His body, this close, calls to me, the connection between us a crackling hum that only we can hear.

His eyes—a shocking, bright blue even in this half lit space—turn me inside out when they dip to take in the faint red mark on my neck.

"That's mine."

Holy. Shit.

I'm not actually going to faint, am I?

His low voice sets off another rush of conversation. All I notice is the heaviness it's dropped right in my middle, the excitement fizzing out to my limbs.

I nod. It's the best I can do.

The place goes silent when he leans in close, traces his nose over the bite he gave me, and up to my ear, scattering goosebumps in his wake like hot sparks. "You want to try this?" he growls and then seems to reconsider his words. "Do you want...me?"

Out in the light, he means, where the whole world can see.

Oh God, he's flayed himself open, right here, in front of everyone. Making an offer I could very well decide to refuse.

My inhalation is a ridiculous, shaky thing, barely akin to breathing. I manage a faint "Yes," clear my throat and then say, "Hell, yes."

Like he's barely held himself back and can't wait another second, he dips again, swipes a tongue over his own hot brand and growls so low the sound feels wrenched from his soul, straight from the earth. His hands cup me, grab me, pull me in and hold me close, while that big, deep-rooted body supports my fall and, oh, lord, what a fall it is. I never want it to stop.

His lips skim my jaw, my cheek, then he dives into my mouth, as if it's the only sustenance he'll ever need.

The room disappears. This kiss isn't just mouths meeting, it's tectonic plates clashing, worlds shifting. I lose my footing, but what does that matter when I can lean into this megalith of a man?

And he's not cold, despite the color of his eyes. He's lava, licking hot and urgent at my lips. How can I help but melt into him? Lost to the drag and pull of a kiss that's slowed to something so soft, my heart breaks open right here, in full view of everyone.

I shift back for air and a chance to see his face.

"You're so beautiful." His words are soundless puffs of warmth on my skin. Caresses, like the scratch of his hands, the sweet, dry press of his closed mouth, the slick heat of a tongue I've felt high and tight between my thighs.

The way he licks into me now—all sweetness and hunger—is the most tender touch I've felt in my life.

It takes a while for reality to set in. When I remember where we are and recognize the center-stage position we're in, a hot flush takes me over.

Stretch you wide open in front of a thousand other people. Zed's words come back to me in a rush, only it's Liev who's holding me up and baring my soul to the masses and I want it. *This*, I want this. With him. Liev King, the mysterious overlord, the man above it all. The man I've been meeting in the dark.

There's talking, laughing, some light clapping

around us—from my table, I would guess. I don't care, but Liev's focus shifts behind me for a second before landing back on my face. "Wanna get out of here?"

"Hell, yes," I say, in no way prepared for him to bend down and haul me over his shoulder, one hand firm on my ass, before carrying me out of the dining hall, to thunderous applause.

I'd be embarrassed if it didn't feel so right.

Liev

Something's snapped in my brain. I feel loose and wild. I'm the beast that's been hibernating inside me, but also the man I've so long denied. I charge out of that room full of people into the cooler, darkening night, and drop her feet to the ground. The next moment, I'm on her, pressing her body to the wall.

Each second not touching and tasting and fucking her is killing me. Like scarfing down hotdogs for ten years and getting a big, juicy steak thrown right in front of my nose and not being able to just tear into it, being forced to stop and say grace or some—

"Grace." I laugh against her mouth. My mind's exploding with potential. With joy. Thoughts skewing everywhere. "I want to fuck you right here."

"Just try it," she replies, her chin raised with that already addictive hint of defiance. It's a taunt.

She bites my lip and pulls it taut.

She's a living *dare*, goading me into wanting her more. I'll have to win her again and again and just the thought's edging me closer to coming.

I'll have to work for her, every step of the way. Hunt her down, take her, make her mine over and over and over again.

My hips pin her to the clapboard siding, my hard-as-rock dick aching to spike her to this wall, to keep her here and show everyone that she's mine. My prize.

Better earn her first.

I shudder, my eyesight compressing dark at the edges before expanding again, my heart twisting in its cage.

What I love the most, watching her in what's left of the daylight, is the challenge in her eyes. Grace is not a brat playing games with my heart.

She's a viking waging all-out war.

With a snarl, I pin her to the wall and kiss her hard—the kind of bruising, claiming kiss we'll both feel for days. She gives me back as good as she gets and then—thank you, God—she shoves me away, hard enough to send me spinning back.

In the next split second, she takes off.

I'm right behind her, limbs pumping, blood thrumming through my veins.

People scatter for her, then go stock still when I

race by, mouths dropping open in almost comical shock. Their reactions don't touch me one way or another, don't rub me right or wrong, except that a part of me wants them to see that she's mine. Or she will be when I catch her.

25

Grace

Instinct takes over.

Fight, flight, fuck—this is all of it, a whirlwind of base human urges encased in skin and bones, fueled by hormones.

My brain doesn't guide this sprint through camp. It's pure, unadulterated adrenaline that keeps me from crashing. Holy shit is it freeing. Not good or bad, but wild in a way I've never experienced. More than the thing we did in the dark.

I veer back onto what I think is the path, my steps awkward in flip-flops. I'd have planned better if I'd known.

My vision's gone weird, clear in front and hazy

around the edges, my eyes skipping from one silhouette to the next—tree trunks, flapping leaves, stones on the path, a downed tree. I sail over it, light as air, my lungs full, my breathing erratic. I land, lose a flip-flop, and keep going, my progress loud over the path. I spare a quick thought for poison ivy, which I hope has been cleared out in this new area.

I can't say how far I go or where the hell I wind up or if I've sprained an ankle somewhere along the way. All I know is the fast, frantic rush of escape. And, my God, it's exciting. Scary, and so goddamn real I can't separate fact from fiction.

With breathtaking suddenness, the forest lightens, the ground evens out, the backlit blue of a nearly twilit sky appears overhead. My other shoe flies off, I push harder, struggling to suck in air, missing the forest scent before I've realized it's gone. Grass slides smooth and damp beneath the soles of my frantic feet. The smell's bright and fresh and full of memories.

He's back there. I feel him, though I can't say how far.

I've gone maybe a dozen steps through an open field when I hear him pounding behind me, so close my nape prickles. And then a hand slips into the back of my jeans, gripping the waist. I jolt to a dead stop, try to turn, throw my hands up in front of my face. In seconds, I'm down, on the ground without the full effect of being slammed to my front. His hold, I realize in a far off way, slows my fall, keeping me from taking the brunt of it the way he's done every single time we've been together.

"Don't move." Liev's low, muttered words send everything spiking inside of me. God, I love this part.

I resist. I can't help it. The instinct that made me run, barefoot, without feeling a thing, now pushes me to fight him. And so I do, kicking back when his bulk closes in, twisting when his hands grasp at my wrists, clawing at him, biting. And through it all, he somehow gets a hand under me, wrenches the button of my jeans open and yanks down the zipper, his moves so rough it's probably broken.

My hips are up, the pants pulled down over my butt in a slower, more sensuous version of our first time. He makes a sound behind me, a low growl that has the hairs on my body standing up, along with my nipples. He mutters something under his breath, and shoves the jeans farther, trapping my knees.

"Mine." That's what he's saying. *Mine mine mine*.

Without warning, he lands a slap on my ass—sudden and sharp. I gasp, try to twist up and block him from doing it again. He wrestles me flat on my chest on the earth, my face in the grass, until I twist to look at him.

Oh, he's lovely. No. No, that's not the right word, I guess. It's not a hard word and the man is definitely *hard*, but it's the way my heart feels when I see him. Bright and excited and ready. A flower bloomed and wide open, soaking in the sun's rays.

This is the moment I stop fighting. I'm pretty sure I stop breathing. My heart doesn't beat, as if all of me is suspended. The surreality of blending the two worlds hits me. Daylight and darkness. Real and fantasy.

It seems fitting this should happen in that liminal time after sunset.

I think his eyes must be on me, though he can't possibly see any better than I do in the dark, although with Liev, I have to wonder. But the low growl he lets out is scary and mean and so goddamn hungry I moan. Working together now, we drag my pants to my ankles, then all the way off.

The scrape of his skin against mine is a secret language the two of us share.

There isn't time to think about it, because in the next second, he's on me again, his heft weighing me down. Another smack burns the side of my ass, his rough hand reaches up and under my T-shirt, finding my breast, which he pinches and pulls and flicks, like I'm a toy. He turns me over with quick efficiency—a lion, playing with his victim before a kill.

Lions don't kiss you, though, with slow, sweet pleasure.

His tongue's a soft caress, somehow fucking my mouth, and loving it too.

"Don't stop," I gasp when he pulls away.

"Hold on. Be patient."

After kissing me so thoroughly that I'm boneless,

I'll give him anything he wants. Except maybe patience. There's not a lot of that happening here.

He fiddles with something low down, his bulk pinning me, and then—whoa my God—all the blood rushes to my pelvis. He's there, stiff and hot between my legs, sliding without penetrating.

My heart goes still.

I'm so slick, my arousal feels cold, his cock a brand against me. A slide back, another forward. A slap of his swollen crown to my aching clit. His torso shifts away, leaving me chilled and alone up top, but then one hand goes to my nape and circles it, like a ring. A collar.

The collar concept I've never quite gotten slides into place then—the symbol, but also the sensation. It feels right the way he holds me. Heavy and intransigent and not entirely of my choosing. No. No, that isn't right, I've chosen this. We've woven this thing together. A call and response of our own making.

Like how he shifts and I roll to lift my ass as some kind of offering.

"This what you wanted?" Liev leans in and whispers against my cheek. "A hot cock between your legs, your face in the dirt?"

Yes yes yes. I don't answer. I can't. I am all body, no brain.

Not just anyone. "*Your* cock," I finally manage. "I want you, Liev."

His hips press tight to mine, showing me how deep he could be, then his teeth give my earlobe a mean tug before letting go. "It's gonna hurt. I'm gonna hurt you."

Adrenaline courses through me, or excitement. Whatever that feeling is when your blood's rushing from your belly into your chest and you can't breathe. I smell him—musk, and metal, that soap smell that links us through our rough, clean, art sink hands. I want to turn around and suck him deep. I want to drown in that scent.

I guess that answers the question of whether I truly crave pain or not.

"I might hurt you back," I taunt and he laughs, the movement swaying our bodies like we're on the same wave, in the same boat, floating this wild ocean together.

"Is this weird?" I swivel to face him again.

He goes still, pulls back to look at me. "Definitely."

"I don't mean the sex. I mean this." I wave my hand between our bodies, suddenly hyper aware that we're practically strangers. "This thing where the sex seems more important than, like...dating. Like we're doing it backwards."

Laughing lightly—the warmest sound I've heard in my life—he leans in and nuzzles my throat, my jaw, my ear. "Maybe the others are doing it wrong." He eases back again with a deep grunt. "Spread your legs."

I obey, without hesitation.

His rumbled response is a prize I didn't realize I

wanted. "You're so wet for me, aren't you? Your little cunt's soaking. I'm gonna pound it so good. You want that? Want your pussy destroyed?"

Fears spikes straight back in, makes everything deeper. This isn't lust the way I've known it all my life, it's something that rearranges my insides and leaves me open, gasping, begging, gagging.

When he thrusts this time, the threat is there, in the strength of the move, the near-penetration that should scare me.

Dazed, I realize the dirty talk has covered up the sounds of foil unwrapping, the snap of rubber. "Don't you fucking move, Grace," he says, his voice ragged now, frayed and low and almost metallic. Or is that the smell? My senses have short circuited. Scents and sound and touch have blended together to create a dangerous cocktail of need. In the mix, my name on the air is a drug.

Of course my body takes his words as a challenge. I've never been an easy person, I guess. I buck, pushing him half off me. He growls, his muscles flex.

He's on me, his hands meeting my flailing arms, his heft trapping me, his knees knocking mine apart, his cock there—suddenly there, threatening to push inside—and then he hunches, bringing his face close to mine. "You want my cock, Grace?"

"Yes. Yes, Liev."

He pushes inside.

"I want you."

26

Liev

I BELONG HERE, I think, my cock barely halfway inside her. Not just her body, but out here, in the darkness, the wild, wide open world.

Her pussy clenches around my cock in the kind of demanding embrace I've craved all these years.

My animal shifts, closer to my skin, words and sensations blurring together to become something more like need. Want. Have.

Mine.

She strains—not to get away, I don't think, but part of me takes it as a bid for freedom and my beast rears his head, growling low and mean. "Stay," he says, pummeling her just a little harder, grinding her hips into the cold, damp grass. "Fucking stay."

Her whining is a reply that sounds as feral as my insides feel and, rather than try to shove that wild thing out of the way the way I used to do, I sink into it, let it take over. Every shift, every press, every hard, slow pump feels deeper, wound tighter than before, until I can't just fuck her pussy. I need more. Of everything.

Quickly, I pull out, slither down until my face is between her thighs and go to town licking, biting, snarling my pleasure and hunger out right here in the musky, fragrant core of her. The place where she can't hide how she smells or tastes or how good all of this feels. Her lips are slippery and swollen, her little clit hard enough to grip with my teeth. And suck.

Her squeal sends me higher, tightens my muscles and loosens what inhibitions I've got left.

I'm up now, flipping her over to run my tongue between her ass cheeks. I hold them open, press my face in, and consume. Pull back, bite. She squirms and I turn to the bite the other side. Then again. Sinking my teeth in, hard enough to mark her. More bites. Because I'm a brute and I want every inch of her skin bruised from my body.

Mine. Mine.

Back to her tiny puckered asshole, which I lick and tongue. At the sound of her whimpering, I pull back and spit, wet and hot. Run my fingers through the ooze, mixed with her juices, then press in.

Her groan goes low, turns into a grunt. Not of protest, but surprise, maybe? I allow her a second to adjust to my fingertip and then push deeper, imagining my engorge cock pressing that tight ring open and, fuck… I want that.

"I want your ass."

She groans. A wordless assent?

"Tell me you'll take my cock in this tight little hole."

Another wordless response as I push a second finger inside, to the first knuckle, then deeper.

"Tell me."

"Oh God. Yes. Yes, do it."

"Do what? Say it." I smooth a hand from her hip up to her shoulder, over that bite mark I wish would stay on her neck forever, then back down. "I need consent, baby."

"Fuck me. However you want, Liev. Take me."

"Like an animal," I groan, my cock swelling impossibly bigger, almost painfully hard.

"Yes." Her voice is gruff. Unrecognizable. "Fuck my ass."

I bend down and give her another bite, which makes her hop, startled, with a tiny giggle that I feel deep in my balls. In my chest, too.

"Do it now," she demands.

"You're not ready."

"Do it. I want it to…"

I pause and listen.

"I want it to hurt. I want to feel it."

Rushing now, I give my fingers another deep twist. Bend to spit on her ass and my cock, and pull her up by the hips.

Lining the head up with her, I take a second to breathe in the pine and sap and grass smells of camp, listen to the cicadas in the trees and the hoots of other kinksters, out of sight, though not too far off, and the quick, frantic breathing of the woman I've somehow become obsessed with.

Feeling more alive than I remember being, ever, I press in, just the tiniest bit, rub my rough palm to her soft lower back when she lurches, waiting for her to be ready, to be sure she wants this. Finally, she shimmies towards me. I slide in, slow, steady, so fucking constricted I might pass out.

Throwing back my head, I howl at the sky, the stars, the almost full moon, and feel righter than I have in a lifetime.

27

Grace

This is what it means to let go. To give myself and my body up, to be nothing but pleasure.

Okay. And a little pain.

When his cock first forges into me, there's a low, guttural feeling that makes me grunt like an animal. When he tightens his hands on my wide-spread ass cheeks and pulls them impossibly wider. When he bends forward and licks and kisses and bites me, again and again, all over my neck and shoulders.

It's all pain, I guess. But pain in pursuit of pleasure. And that's something else entirely.

By the time he pulls out and lunges inside me again, I'm letting out a continuous, low sound. An ugly, hummed groan, straight from my belly, my lungs, my throat, into the ground, where it's eaten up my earth. Another vibration to join a million others.

My body's splayed out, stretched wide, an earth-bound offering to the skies or the wind or something bigger than either of us. Life a sacrifice to some ancient god, this pleasure feels tied up in something bigger, wider, deeper than either of us could ever be, apart.

After a long, sucking bite, he lifts up and brings all his concentration to bear on where we're joined. Him inside of me, filling me, making me feel...

"So good. God. God."

With a happy growl, he grips my hips again, hard, and starts pounding in earnest. I don't know if I'll come from this. I don't care. But I feel my insides constricting, my empty pussy trying, trying so hard to clench on something. Anything. I struggle to get a hand down under my body, between my legs, where I touch my clit and—

"Oh shit. I'm coming. I'm coming."

"Fuck, yes," he mutters. "Do it. Come all over my cock."

Oh wow. That does it. Filthy words and a smack on my ass and then...just as I curl forward, every muscle tight, tight, tight from the orgasm to end all orgasms, he covers my body with his heavy one, grabs my breasts, and uses them—uses me—to bring himself to climax.

"You're fucking mine," he rumbles, as fiercely savage as he's ever sounded. "All of you."

And then he's gone, replaced by the cruel,

vicious, snapping beast he becomes when he lets it all out.

I want to see him while he comes, I realize, as my body cuts off all blood flow to my brain.

Someday, I want to see his face.

Someday.

With a final huff, Liev King collapses heavily on top of me, making me sprawl boneless on the cold, gritty ground.

And it's everything I ever wanted.

28

Liev

There's nothing like bringing your woman home for the first time.

In theory.

Right now, despite just having had the best sex of my life, I'm seeing potential issues.

First of all, aside from Lamé and Zion, I've had no one over. I can't imagine what she'll think of the place.

"What are we doing out here?" she asks when we've settled on the front porch steps.

"I've probably got some explaining to do."

"Why?" Her eyes narrow. "We just met. You don't have to explain anything."

Those words don't feel good, even if they are the cold, honest truth.

"I might not owe you an explanation. But..." I twist to look over my shoulder at my closed front door. "Fuck it. Come on."

Standing, I grab her hand and draw her inside.

I push a switch. The foyer light comes on, illuminating a world that was mostly Helen's, now dulled by time and disuse.

Grace's eyebrows rise as she takes it all in—the delicate antique wooden table by the front door, the wavy-glassed mirror, a series of vintage bird prints on the wall.

"*You* live here?" Grace just looks puzzled now, as if trying to work out a calculation in her head and coming up with the wrong solution every time. "This doesn't look like you. At all."

I don't ask how she could possibly know that. From day one, our connection's been inexplicably deep.

"I live here. Kind of." It's weird to open up and admit how mixed up I've been. "The house always seemed more Helen's than mine. I've made progress in the past year. Got rid of a few things. Got it cleaned." I look towards the staircase. "Still don't sleep in our room."

"She's been gone how long?"

"Three years."

She nods.

I don't know who reaches out first, but we're

holding hands when we walk into the next room. "Living room," I say unnecessarily.

She moves into the space with a slow respect that turns my lust into something so close to love I can't tell them apart.

Swallowing back the need to tell her, I tighten my hold and lead her on. We go through every room in the house. There are still bits of Helen here and there, though I've given a lot of it away over the past year. It makes for a house that's pretty empty in places. Like it's been waiting.

In the master bedroom, Grace picks up a dusty picture of the two of us. We're sitting on the river in two separate inner tubes, burned bright red and smiling like dumbasses. I love that picture. "She was beautiful."

"Yeah."

"I'm...I don't know how to manage this, Liev."

"What?"

"The way I feel for you, so suddenly. And..." She indicates the room. "Your loss. All this."

"I'm kinda figuring things out myself, to be honest."

"I'm glad you brought me here."

"You sure? Not too much?"

"I lost my dad a few years ago." She puts the photo down, gently. Runs a finger over the top of the frame in a final caress. "We didn't have time to let him go like this, bit by bit. We moved Mom out, sold the house."

"Shit, Grace. I'm sorry."

"Thanks." She shrugs, her eyes big and sad. "Can I see your studio?"

"Sure. Come on." Our footsteps quick, we clatter downstairs. I grab a big, tarnished candelabra from the dining room and matches in the kitchen, then lead her out the back door, to the studio. Instead of putting on the overhead, I light the wicks and set it down on my work table. "Have a seat." I indicate the sofa and go to the fridge for some beers.

I'm nervous as I settle beside her, but these nerves are good clean first date nerves as opposed to the kind you get from baring all the skeletons in your closet.

We kiss and make out for a bit, all of it more casual than anything we did out in the wild. I like her this way, too.

"So, Grace." I pull back, my breath shaky, let my arm hang out over her shoulders and pull her close to my side. She feels good against me. "Tell me something about yourself."

"We've done this whole thing backwards." Her giggle is low and rough and a little broken in places. Fuck, it warms my soul. "Okay. Uh... I'm a Scorpio."

I snort. "Astrology?"

"Not into it? Whatever, dude. You literally chase women in the woods in order to have your way with them." I poke her in the ribs, aching to hear another of her laughs. "Hey!" This one's higher, fainter. It's cute as hell.

"You didn't seem to mind, Grace."

"I don't know, old man. One of us could've had an eye out."

Halfway through a sip, my eyes slide her way. "Nah ah. No. Don't you dare start that. I've got enough with Lamé. I'll get a complex if it becomes a thing."

"A thing." Chin raised a little, as if she's holding something in, she looks around the room. I get the feeling she's avoiding my eyes, but that can't be right. I see the moment her gaze finds the sculpture of us. "Are *we* a thing, Liev?"

"God, I hope so." The answer rushes out of me, all feeling and brute honesty. Shoving back the embarrassment trying to edge its way in, I lean over and put down my beer, turn towards her and reach out. She wedges her can between her thighs and slides her hands into mine. I'm shocked anew at the feel of calluses on her fingers. That's not something I've felt too often on someone else. I grasp her hands and turn them over. "How'd you get these?"

After a puzzled second, she replies. "I'm a painter. A house painter."

My brows drop. "You're not an artist?"

"A lot of people have asked that this week."

"With good reason. Your stuff's good."

She stares at something—maybe the five flames dancing in front of us. "So, you want my story?"

"Up to you." I give her hand a squeeze.

"My dad's the one who pushed me to pursue the

art thing. I mean, I wanted to, but he made sure I *could*. Six years ago, everything changed."

"What happened?"

"Mom and Dad went out to dinner. Date night. Dad's night to drink, Mom drove." I recognize the smile on her face. It's the one you wear to soften a story you've told too many times. "She had a stroke, less than a mile from the house. Lost control of the car. It flipped. Dad...was gone. She had another stroke three years ago. Another last year." I use our joined hands to tuck her in again, pressed into my side. "I left school. Didn't graduate. Vanessa, my big sister, was pregnant at the time, with her second kid. She helps out, but...I'm basically it for Mom, you know? I work and take care of her and make sure she gets to appointments. That kind of thing makes you grow up pretty fast." She pulls from my grasp and holds her palm out.

There's a tightly-closed rosebud inked in the middle. It reminds me of old etchings in one of my old Art History books. It's frankly stunning.

"This is for him. Dad. Or more for me, I guess. Cause I miss him." She throws me a glance. "He called me his little Rosebud. Pretty as a rose and twice as thorny. He always joked that you had to fight through the thorns to get the real me."

"I like the thorns. Sure that's not the real you?"

Her wide-eyed gaze meets mine. Attraction sparks between us, shockingly bright in the candles' low glow. "Maybe so."

"How's your mom now?"

"Recovery's slow. And we're constantly worried it'll happen again."

"And you just work? Take care of her. Pay bills."

"There's lots of debt. College debt, medical bills. Lots and lots of those. Yeah. I work."

"And come to Camp Haven."

She shakes with a laugh. "Max made me come. She paid for it, arranged for Vanessa to stay with Mom. It's my birthday present."

"She's a good friend."

"The best."

A thought occurs to me. "Where do you live?"

"Couple hours south."

"That's not too far."

"Right." She sounds skeptical.

"I'll visit you. If you want."

"Really?" Her smile's bright. "Yeah. Yeah, I'd like that."

My chest warms. "Okay. Um, last name?"

"Grace Evelyn Dubois."

"You're missing a Rosebud in there."

Her sigh is deep and content and it gives me that feeling I used to get when I'd wake up on Sunday mornings with nothing to do but be. I want to stretch my limbs and sigh.

"What's your last name, sculptor man?"

"Oh, uh. King."

She stiffens. "Holy shit."

"What?"

"You're Liev King. *The* fucking Liev King?"

I swallow back my discomfort and hope she can't see my flushed face. "I might be."

"No wonder. No *wonder* you're so good." Laughing, she points at my new work. "I mean. That one? The one of us? When did you start that? Like yesterday?"

"The night we met."

"Met. Is that the word for what we did that night?"

I lean down and put my lips to the crown of her head, breathe her in. "I don't think there is a word for it. For us."

"You're probably right." She sighs, long and deep.

"So." I'm a little nervous, suddenly, but I have to ask. "Speaking of us. What's next?"

"I don't know. Truly, I..."

"I have to ask you something, Grace. Or tell you. Or... It's serious."

"Okay." Our conversation's edged so far into the deep that her hesitation's no surprise.

"First off, I'm in therapy, just so you know."

"Okay, that's good. Me, too." Her shoulder lifts. "When I can afford it."

"So, if you...we... *Okay*." I shut my eyes and get my thoughts straightened out. "My relationship with Helen was complicated. We didn't always want the same things. I got jealous. Needlessly. It was unhealthy and unfair to her. It ate at our relationship, gnawed away at my insides. Hollowed me out." It's hard to keep my voice flat, but I work at it. "Then, one day, she was *dying*."

"Liev, you don't need to—"

"I do."

Grace nods, her head bumping my chin. She doesn't turn around. I appreciate the privacy.

"The jealousy was so petty. So pointless compared to losing her. "I inhale, let it out, lower my mouth and press it to her hair. "Sorry. I don't know what I'm trying to say."

She turns just enough so I can see a tear gather at the edge of her eye. It gets fatter and fatter until it overflows, laying a shiny trail to the corner of her mouth. I lift my hand to wipe it off and stop. It seems wrong suddenly to erase someone else's sorrow. Just because I can't stand to see her cry doesn't mean she doesn't get to.

My hand's still hovering when she leans in and presses her tearstained cheek right to it, smearing the wetness against me, sharing her heartache and maybe accepting a measure of mine.

"So, how do you feel about monogamy?" I'm holding my breath.

"Honestly?"

"Yes."

"I wouldn't want to share you," she says, her voice a low growl that sends warmth and shivers up my spine. "*Ever*."

"Good." Relieved, I slip my fingers into her hair

and pull her head back, watching the way her eyes glow warm and hungry. "Me neither."

I want to take her, right here in my lair.

I lean in to stroke my nose up her damp cheek, scenting her, letting her feel the threat and the weight of these feelings I've somehow already developed for her. "Do me a favor, will you, Rosebud?"

"Okay."

"Will you give this a try? Us? It'll be hard. I'm a pain in the ass and I've got growing to do and you're two hours away, with your own..."

"Responsibilities."

"Exactly. But this..." *Chemistry, craving, connection.* "This *thing* between us. I think it's worth the effort. It's worth a try."

She twists in my arms and cups my face with those strong, capable hands, drawing so close I have to lean in to hear her whisper. "We're totally worth it, Liev." She touches her nose to mine. "I'm all in. I'm yours."

With a groan, I press my lips to hers and breathe her in, this scent made just for me. Or maybe I'm the one made to her specifications? God, I hope so. I really fucking hope so.

EPILOGUE

Grace

Eleven and a half months later...

"That looks amazing." I walk up behind Liev and wrap my arms around his strong chest, lean in and sway a little, giving him all my weight, taking a little of his in the process. It's how we roll—a little you, a little me. It's always a fight. And it's always worth it.

"You think?" He cants his head, eyeing the sculpture's placement at the edge of our woods, along with the plaque, bearing its name: *Wherever we fall.*

"I love it." I rub my face against his shoulder blade. "I love all of it."

He breathes in a deep, nervous breath and claps his hands. "Think we've got time for a—" He casts a laughing glance at our spot in the woods, knowing full well we've got our first ever annual general meeting to get to. Like, right now.

"Stop it. I know you can't wait to get things started."

"I know." He grabs my hand and we head off to the main building together, both eager to see what the rest of the new Camp Haven Co-operative's members see in our future.

From what we've heard, everyone's really excited. And Liev, I know, is happy to retire from his position as Overlord.

The new camp's starting tonight, right after the meeting, and I just know it'll be wild.

We enter through the big front doors and say hello to the big group of kinksters—mostly in street clothes, still—milling around drinking coffee and shooting the shit before things kick off. The atmosphere's the same as last year, as far as I can tell—all that friendly, openness is right there at the forefront, so much of it focused on Liev who's smiling and open and so happy it pinches my heart.

I mean, yeah, I've got a lot to do with that happiness, just like he's got a lot to do with mine. The man's my other half, my soulmate. He's my rock and I'm so fucking proud to be his I've inked him into my skin. My wolf. Not a loner anymore.

He's smiling and hugging a guy named Sledge,

who used to be a friend, long ago. He's got hundreds of friends here today. Over a thousand. The love pouring out is just epic. We'll move mountains, all together. I can feel it.

Max winds her arm around my waist and pulls me tight. "So. Just one time, right? Fuck him once, get it out of your system."

I bump my hip to hers. "You were right, I was wrong."

"I know, I know," she singsongs. "You look happy."

"You know I am."

"You gonna show me the tattoo parlor, or what?"

"Oh my God, you're gonna love it, Max. It's so…"

"You?"

"Us."

She looks around. "You and Liev?

I shake my head and look around and the colors and shapes and sizes and genders, all mixed up in a big, happy mess. "All of us. This."

"It's only right." Her expression's full of a tight-lipped, teary-eyed pride. "Saw your mom today."

"What do you think of her place?"

"It's adorable."

"She's happy."

"Best of both worlds, right? She's got you right next door."

"With her own space."

"And the cottage is so her."

"I know." I look over at Liev, immediately heating

at the sight of those big arms, slung over another man's back. I won't share—ever—but I've certainly fantasized him as a gruff gladiator more than once. I've even role-played being his hard-won prize a time or two. It was dirty and delicious. "I'm so lucky."

Max, who's between partners right now, lets out a long, mournful sigh. "You know. You really are. First time at camp, you just show up all innocent and wide-eyed and *Oh, I'm only doing it once* and here you are actually living at—"

"Let's get started everyone!" Lamé calls out in their boss voice as they skate out of the back office, a laptop in their hand. I don't have to look at Liev to see him rolling his eyes. Lamé's wearing what appear to be fishnet pants on the bottom and, up top, a T-shirt that has me laughing my ass off the whole way to the meeting room. QUEEN OF FUCKING EVERYTHING is written across the chest in giant, pink, sparkling letters.

After settling into our chairs, Lamé leads the meeting with incredible—but unsurprising—efficiency. It's quick and fun and feels like the right thing. Liev, who's got his arm around my shoulders, clearly agrees.

We wrap it up and start the evening's festivities. Lamé disappears, no doubt to change into something much more extravagant. Liev's just leaned in with that look he gets when he's in the mood to chase me down, when we're jostled from behind. "Oh my God you guys," Lamé's voice is low and urgent. Their skin looks grey which, considering their usual sepia-brown tone, is not okay.

They hold out their phone. Immediately, I panic, wanting to pull my own phone out to check for messages. Mom's emergency tone didn't sound, though, so that's not probably not the issue. "What? What is it?"

"Look."

I grab their hand to still the shaking and peer at the screen for a few seconds before the words make any sense.

When they do, my stomach drops.

Zion Mason kinky sex scandal rocks the entertainment world.

Below that, I see the words *sadist* and *sexual free-for-all*. There's a photo of his wife, clearly running from the paps—oh my God, that's a whole other story—and below that, every single lurid term you can imagine.

This is bad. This is really, really bad.

"Where is he now?"

"I don't know," Lamé says in a hush. "Before this all happened, he told me he'd make it by next week. He had some red carpet events first. What do we do? I don't know what to do. I always know what to do. I don't know here. I don't know."

Liev and I share a look, knowing this same thing could happen to him, though a sculptor's notoriety probably wouldn't suffer the same way. Hell, it could even up the price of his stuff.

Besides, he only plays with me.

However, when wholesome movie stars with hit series, award nominations, and a pretty, young wife get caught doing very dirty things? Yeah, they fall long and they fall really, really hard.

"Let's go get our boy," Liev says in that sure, solid way.

"Yeah." I look around at the motley-ass family I've become part of and nod up at the guy I share my body and heart and soul with and I just know, in this moment, that we'll figure this out, together. "Let's go."

THE END

Read Grace and Liev's Bonus Epilogue here: https://dl.bookfunnel.com/f3cyjdbiyo

Read on for a sneak peek of POSSESSION, available now!

WHEREVER WE FALL

A CAMP HAVEN BONUS EPILOGUE

1

Liev

I'M LOSING MY SHIT. Not talking a little anxiety here, I'm talking about staring right into the flames before jumping into the inferno. The moment it all comes down to. Right here, out by the Primal Fire circle, where a few dozen campers are getting revved up for the big hunt, I'm losing every bit of cool I ever had.

I'm doing it tonight. I'm asking her. This is probably the worst idea I've ever had.

Someone smacks me on the shoulder. I turn, unsurprised to see Zion, smirk in place. "You look like you're gonna lose your dinner, man."

"Might."

"Ah, hell. You serious?" He wraps his arm around my shoulders and squeezes. "She's gonna say yes."

"Says the guy whose wife wouldn't speak to him."

"My fake wife." He straightens away from me, looks over to where the prey are milling around and tightens up a like a coiled spring.

"Whatever," I say, although seeing him so messed up over her definitely helps. Call me an asshole, but at least I knew my woman was *mine*. Poor bastard didn't even realize he's been lusting after that one for months. He even put a damn ring on her finger. "She's not doing this, is she?" I nod towards the group.

His jaw goes so tight I'm frankly worried for his movie star teeth. "I don't know. The way things have been going... Probably."

"She do orientation?"

"Yes. You know. The kidnapping?"

"Oh, right." Can I help it that the grin that takes over my face is a little evil? "Better run fast, I guess." I'm taunting him, I know. After all his years of doing everything and everyone at camp, it's some kind of justice that the Sexiest Man Alive can only get it up for the wife who runs him ragged.

Someone yells and my heart trips into gear. Beside me, Zion goes rigid. Man, I hope this thing with Twyla doesn't kill him.

I stare hard at the tightly grouped prey—mostly pups and ponies—and finally locate Grace. She's the stillest person there, I note as her long, lean form comes into focus. If I didn't know how excited she is to be in her first Big Hunt, I'd say she looks...calm, almost. Unaffected.

The opposite of me. Except now, seeing her like that, my energy's changing. Instead of anxious, I'm revved. I'm ready.

Someone yells. Everything goes quiet.

I shut my eyes and let the sounds and smells of people and nature and the night take over.

When the warning horn blows, scattering the participants, my heartbeat spikes into overdrive. Alongside the other predators, I wait another 10 seconds for the second starting signal—this one a shot —and I'm off.

Running hard, lungs and heart, arms and legs pumping. Eyes shifting left to right, until I spot her in the distance, wearing a glow in the dark yellow bracelet that tells others she's off-limits.

Because she's *mine*.

Cicadas hum all around, a low, constant bass rhythm to this wild adventure. To my right, someone screams, a voice howls from the woods. Branches snap, flesh slaps flesh. It's pure, feral mayhem out here, full of animal sounds and earthy smells and the strains of instincts unleashed. I know where she's going now. I didn't, at first, but there's nowhere else she'd go head in this direction. This is perfect. Like I wrote it myself.

She looks back and sees me, her features invisible, but her body moving fast and frantic. She races forward again and stumbles, right beside the lake. I put on a burst of speed. Almost there. Push harder. My feet sink deep into the sandy beach, my steps slow, she turns, her eyes huge, frightened.

I put on a burst of speed. Close. Close. Near enough that I hear her quick, frantic gasps, I feel them deep in my balls.

She swerves towards the water, then away. That's when I leap.

The moment my body touches her—the capture—is indescribable. Pure rightness. A dance, a song, a prayer.

We land a little harder than we've done in the past, but the soft sand helps cushion us. She fights, hard, kicking my shoulder, just missing my face, turns and crawls straight towards the water.

She's just gotten to her feet again when I wrap an arm around her middle and lift her clear off the ground.

Oh, fuck do I love the way she fights back—no half-measures here—she's full-speed, full-strength, the way she is in everything. It's one of the many things I love about her. Us.

It takes every bit of power I have to get a good grip and hold her tight, but when I do, she makes that *sound*...and it's all worth it. The bruises, the exhaustion. The fucking worry that she'll say no.

Shit. None of that.

Breathing hard, I get her down and cover her. She's on her back—probably better in the sand—and she's still fighting, but the fight's almost a caress now. Every twist is foreplay, every bite is a slow stroke to my cock. She'll be soaking wet when I touch her.

I can't wait a second longer.

I lean down, snag her lip between my teeth and pull gently.

She stops moving except for the most minute lift of her hips. "Got you, baby."

She laughs, low and warm. "For now."

That's as good of a cue as I'll ever get, isn't it?

"For always."

"You *wish*." She arches back, trying to rid herself of me again, but I know this trick. I'm not falling for it tonight.

"I do." I cage her in with my arms, push my pelvis to hers, letting her feel all the want in my body, while the full moon's light shows her the stark craving in my heart. "I want you forever."

Her eyes narrow, questioning. "You're gonna have to fight me for that."

I grin. "I know."

2

Grace

Something's going on here tonight. Something not part of the plan. I can't tell if Liev's just really worked up about this hunt—like I am—or if it's something else.

He reaches down and wrenches up my skirt, scrapes that rough hand up my thigh, and finds me bare and wet underneath. His eyes shut with the kind of long, slow sigh I've become addicted to hearing. It's like a shared skipped heartbeat out here in the thrumming, moving night. A moment of purity between us.

"Is this mine, Grace?" He cups my pussy, the move so possessive I shiver.

"I don't know. Is it?" Even splayed out for his pleasure like this, I can't help that hint of challenge in my voice. It's what we do, after all. It's who we are. I feed him, he feeds me.

"You know it is."

"Do I?" I kick up, but he's got my number. One heavy leg is right there, weighing hard on both of mine. His face looks positively evil. Possessive and powerful. I shake when he parts me with the pads of his no-nonsense fingers and opens up my pussy like he owns it. And, oh fuck... the way his finger slides right in, fucking into me in the way that squeezes my eyes shut and curls up my spine—I want him to own me. I want to be his, all his, all the time. "Yes," I gasp. "Yes."

He goes harder, somehow, around the jaw, his eyes glinting hard, reminding me of how they looked in a ski mask. When he was still my stranger.

He works me hard, G-spot and clit—his face almost grim while he does it and, oh, that mean expression brings me so close to coming I almost cry when he pulls away. But his cock's right there, teasing and then pressing into my aching, empty core, and I'm whole again.

He takes his time in bed at home, but out here, he's bestial: slow so as not to hurt me, but brutish. His hard cock opens me up, stretching me as full as I've ever been, each thrust a punishment, a claiming. I moan when he shifts back, lifts up my hips and pounds harder, his glittering eyes caught on the action, his hands holding me tight.

"Give me your hand."

"What?" My vision's fuzzy and I'm so close to coming I can't make sense of his words.

"Your hand. Let me have it."

I reach up, palm towards him. He drops something warm and hard inside it and closes my fingers over it, tight. "Marry me," he gasps, throwing back his head and shutting his eyes the way he does when he's close. A rumbling—barely sound—starts deep in his chest.

He's hammering hard into me now, his cock so big I cringe when he bottoms out, the slap of his balls loud in the night. He pulls back a little. "You okay?" He runs a hand down my still-outstretched arm in a gentle caress, slowing his pace, his face suddenly worried.

I feel the hard, round edge of metal in my palm, a sharp prick. Stone?

Oh my God. Oh my God. Tears hit my eyes before I've even felt them.

"Yes." Like my tears, the word's out in the air before my brain's caught up with the rest of me. Always, with him, my body knows first. The world loses more focus, the moon and stars blur and go spikey.

He stops moving entirely, his hands still possessive on my body. "Yes you're okay or yes you'll take my hand in marriage?"

"Yes." Crying harder now, I smile. "Yes to all of it. Yes. I'll marry you."

"Yeah? You'll be mine?" He sucks in a long, slow breath and looks up at the sky again. I get the feeling he's thanking all those celestial bodies the way I have every time I've been out here with him. Every day since the night we came together.

His ass tightens, pushing him farther inside me. I can't help but clench around him, so fully in the moment that I forget about the rough sand and the smell of lake water and the heavy ring in my hand.

"Here." Another slow thrust, this one deep, sensuous. He opens my fingers, takes the ring and offers it up to my other hand.

It all takes a minute, given how overcome I am. Finally he slides it on, his dick slicking into me with perfect synchronicity, and—oh God, I'm there. I'm already there! My body tightens, arches back, my eyes shut out everything but the friction of skin to skin, and I come hard on his cock.

He's right there a few sloppy thrusts later, pressing in hard once, then again, his cock bare, his orgasm voiced with a howl in the night. Others reply, like a pack of wolves calling from afar.

I don't feel my body for a long handful of seconds. I'm air. Rushing blood, then loose muscles, liquid bones.

By the time I come down, he's wrapped his legs around me and hauled me up to sitting on his lap. He kisses me hard—as much a stamp of ownership as the ring on my finger—pulls away and trails his gaze over my face.

"You sure? Not just the hormones talking?"

"I'm sure. And, yes it's the hormones. But, you know. These sex chemicals have not guided me wrong thus far, so..." I lean in and kiss him, this time soft and easy, showing him just how much time we have to love one another. "The answer's yes. Yes, yes, I want to marry you."

His forehead drops to mine, his nose nudges my face, he drags in my scent, nips at my jaw, my ear. He smells so good like this, outside, a little sweaty, with the breeze off the lake and the musk of our bodies blending together.

"I love you, Rosebud. Not just in the dirt, in the dark, in the dead of night, but all the time. Always. In all the ways."

I sing a light hum in response. "I love you, too, Liev."

And I do. I love him. My animal, my man. My primal mate.

He's starting to harden inside me. I'm exhausted, but I can't help tightening around him, just a little, just to test this connection once more.

"You gonna run this time?" he asks, just barely circling his hips.

"I don't know. You gonna chase me?"

He grins flat-out, which isn't something he used

to do. The knowledge curls warm in my chest. "I'll always chase you, Rosebud. Always."

Read on for a sneak peek of POSSESSION, Zion and Twyla's story...

POSSESSION

Zion

I'm about to kidnap my wife.

No, that's not a euphemism. And no, it's not a joke.

But we're playing here, acting out just one of her many—it turns out—fantasies.

Doing it with a stranger: check. Impact play: check. Pushing every one of her limits: check.

I've yet to find the thing my wife doesn't want and I'll tell you, keeping up with her is killing me. In a good way.

Mostly.

Something snaps under my foot and I go still. Blade, the person I've handpicked to be my wingman, stops beside me. I've known him for years. He's quiet and dependable. Steady and solid and up for just about anything.

Around us, the woods are busy, loud, teeming

with life and sounds and the smells you get when it hasn't rained in way too long. There's a heaviness to the air, like maybe a storm's coming.

I hope so. Anything to relieve the tension that's been building since my wife got here.

"That her?" asks Blade, indicating a hint of color shifting between the trees up ahead.

I nod, staring hard at the shocking red of her dress as we set off again, quieter now, careful not to give ourselves away.

The closer we get, the more details I can make out—the dress looks like something Marilyn Monroe would've worn, low cut with a nipped in waist and a skirt that fluffs out all around her. That's where the resemblance ends. She's bigger than Monroe, her curves fuller, softer, her hair a rich, dark brown, and her skin the color of warm sand. She looks like a polka dotted cake and I want to devour every curve and dimple and scar on that sweet, round body. I want to lick her smooth skin and bite into those thick thighs, while my fingers twist into that mound of loose, dark curls. I want to make her squirm.

I'm shocked at how on edge I am going into this. I don't get nervous. Not here, at camp, and not when it comes to my body.

Now that Twyla's in the picture, though, I'm nothing but nerves. There's a whole useless, messed up bundle of them writhing in my gut. Fear and excitement so tightly entwined I'm not sure I'll ever figure out which is which.

Up ahead, she moves a step closer and I come to a sudden stop, close my eyes, breathe in, deep. Beside me, Blade waits. Finally, when I've gotten back at least a little of my normal calm, I look at him and nod. "Definitely her."

How do I know?

I'd recognize her anywhere. Her smell, her taste, and those little sounds she makes. I picture those warm, brown eyes, unfocused in pleasure.

Her shape's clear—short and thick, with tiny ankles and knees and wrists, her waist cinched in and the rest of her gorgeously plush. I want to spread her apart and press my face into all that goodness.

I'm dying to play with her again, even though I had her just this morning.

And the thing about Twyla is that, though her beauty's undeniable, it's the rest of her that pulls me in—her mind, her heart, her sweet, sinful soul.

"Just look at all that," I say, unable to hold my admiration inside.

Blade grins. He knows better than to dwell too long on how good my wife looks, traipsing around in that puffy little dress, those dimpled thighs just begging to be bruised, her throat already showing marks where I held her.

All consensual of course. Everything we've done this week's been just dandy with her—my sweet, clueless little newbie.

The irony in this whole wild thing is that I'm the experienced one and yet, I'm the one who's been torn apart by it. Every exchange, every interaction's shown me that I can't control myself when it comes to Twyla Hernandez. I'm the one who hungers and wants and chases, while she—

Bends down and picks a flower, brings it to her nose and sniffs.

"She's so cute, man. I'm jealous." Blade throws me a grin that I'd wipe off his face if I didn't need him.

Because Twyla—the woman I married not for love, but for appearances—didn't want just one man to take her and make her do unspeakable things. She wanted two.

That decision alone was a message. A bratty, little nose-snubbing that resonates deep in my bones.

"She's mine," I tell him. It's a warning. A promise. A threat.

"I know, man."

He can touch her, today, but that's it.

Her head tilts at the sound of my voice, though I'm not sure she can actually hear me from the clearing. She doesn't have to, though, not with the connection we've got. She could say my name from a mile away and I swear, I'd break into a sweat.

I don't look at Blade when I start moving again, and I don't wait to make sure he's beside me. He either is or he isn't. Doesn't matter.

"Mine," I growl as we stalk my sweet little wife, giving her exactly what she wants. "She's mine."

All that matters is Twyla. Now, forever, always.

Thank you so much for reading this book. If you enjoyed it, please consider reviewing or recommending it to others so they can find it, too!

Keep in touch through one of the links below.

Newsletter: www.adrianaanders.com/newsletter
Bookbub: www.bookbub.com/profile/adriana-anders
Facebook: facebook.com/adrianaandersauthor
Join my reader group: facebook.com/groups/booksmarttarts
Follow me on Instagram: instagram.com/adriana.anders
Tweet with me: twitter.com/adrianasboudoir

ACKNOWLEDGEMENTS

Hello lovely reader!

Oh, it's been a rough couple of years, hasn't it? I know I got bogged down in life and family stuff and found myself totally unable to write this book the way I wanted.

I've been wanting to tell this story for a few years now but everything I was writing was too introspective, too much a journey of self-discovery and not the sexy times I'd promised. In the end, I can't even say how or why, but it finally just...popped out. That's the way with writing, I guess. At least for me.

In any case, I want to thank you, my readers, for bearing with me while I pried this book out of my brain. It's been a tough journey, but I'm so happy to have made it and even happier that you came along for the ride. Of course, now that it's out, I can safely say that there will be more Camp Haven books. Zion, as you already know, has a story just bubbling its way from my subconscious onto the page. Max will absolutely get her time in the sun, too. And there are others. Many, many others. So if you love these characters and their stories and you enjoy this wild and idealistic place where anything goes, please give the world a shout about Kink Camp: Hunted and the Camp Haven series.

In the meantime, I must absolutely thank one person in particular. The woman who kept me in front of my computer, typing, come hell or high water, over the last year and a half: Alleyne Dickens. You are a good friend, an excellent writing partner and, quite frankly, one of the most talented authors I know. Thank you for being there.

To Kimberly Cannon, editor extraordinaire: you are an absolute angel to have stuck with me all year. I've been flaky and a mess and you've been so patient with me. Bless you!!! Leigh Kramer: huge, mega thanks for reading this book with your smart, sensitive eye. You are a godsend. Your feedback was perfect. Another big thank you goes to Madeline Iva, who gave me the impetus I needed to get to the very end.

Other folks who helped me push this big baby out into the world are Sofie Couch, and Joanna Bourne whose presence in those zoom calls helped me show up day by day.

Finally, thank you to Molly O'Keefe for your perfect feedback and your kind words. You are, as always, on point, my friend.

Thanks to Natasha Snow for making not one, but two gorgeous covers for this book. I adore them both.

Et merci, Arnaud. Je t'aime.

Okay my friends. That's it for now. Until next time, happy reading!!!!

ALSO BY ADRIANA ANDERS

Camp Haven/Kink Camp Series

Possession

Paris Je t'Aime Series

We'll Never Have Paris

The French Kiss-Off (coming soon)

The Survival Instincts Series

Deep Blue

Whiteout

Uncharted

Love at Last Series

Loving the Secret Billionaire

Loving the Wounded Warrior

Loving the Mountain Man

The Blank Canvas Series

Under Her Skin

By Her Touch

In His Hands

Standalone

Daddy Crush

ABOUT ADRIANA ANDERS

Adriana Anders is the award-winning author of Romantic Suspense, Contemporary, and Erotic Romance. Her debut, Under Her Skin, was a Publishers Weekly Best Book of 2017 and double recipient of the HOLT Medallion award. Whiteout was named a Bookpage Best Book of the Year, an Entertainment Weekly Top 10 Romance, and an OprahMag Best Romance of 2020. Her books have received critical acclaim from the New York Times, OprahMag, Entertainment Weekly, Booklist, Bustle, USA Today Happy Ever After, Book Riot, Romantic Times, Publishers' Weekly, and Kirkus, amongst other publications. Today, she resides with her husband and two children on the coast of France, writing the love stories of her heart. Visit Adriana's Website for her current booklist: adrianaanders.com

- bookbub.com/profile/adriana-anders
- x.com/AdrianasBoudoir
- instagram.com/adriana.anders
- pinterest.com/adrianasboudoir
- facebook.com/adrianaandersauthor
- tiktok.com/@adrianaanders

Printed in Dunstable, United Kingdom